Everything That Could Not Happen Will Happen Now

A Novel
By
Alberto Ramirez

FLORICANTO PRESS

FLORICANTO™ Press

7177 Walnut Canyon Rd.

Moorpark, California 93021

(415) 793-2662

www.FLORICANTOPRESS.com

ISBN: 978-1537753591

"Por nuestra cultura hablarán nuestros libros. Our books shall speak for our culture."

Roberto Cabello-Argandoña, Editor

Leyla Namazie, co-editor

Everything That Could Not Happen Will Happen Now

For my father and mother (Ito & Ita)

1

I'm living in a foreign land.

Juan dog-eared the page of the *Norton Anthology of English Literature* that he'd been reading and laid the book on the little table, beside the old Hermes typewriter with the jammed type bars. It was nearly midnight and the students in the upstairs dorm-room were drinking again. It was their regular, Thursday night ritual. In observance of the rigors of academic life, they started their weekend early. Through the ceiling he could hear their heavy footsteps, drunken laughter and slurred conversations, loud and cheerful.

If Juan wasn't already losing his mind it might have driven him crazy. He picked up the book again and continued reading silently.

Then the fierce spirit painfully endured hardship for a time, he who dwelt in the darkness, for every day he heard loud mirth in the hall.

Upstairs somebody broke a bottle and he stopped reading again, scowled and grumbled at the high, whitewashed ceiling.

I'm living in a foreign land.

This thought, like a trapped wasp, stung him over and over and, in an effort to squash it, he read from *Beowulf* aloud.

"Then, after night came, Grendel went to survey the tall house; how, after their beer drinking, they felt no sorrow, no misery of men."

The sound of the revelers grew louder, as a drunken student started boasting about his intellectual prowess: "I'm going to get perfect scores on midterms, because I'm a genius!"

Accustomed as he'd become to the noise, this particular student's voice was so grating that he couldn't go on studying tonight. He put the anthology down on the floor and turned off the banker's lamp. And once the lights went out, a horde of paranoid thoughts came rushing into his tired mind. There was something about the darkness that brought them out into the open, like cockroaches. Sitting at the edge of the bed, he closed his eyes, braced himself and let them run their course.

First a childish poem to honor the upstairs neighbors, half-remembered and half-invented:

From the high plateau, where he could not go, a voice called out to him below: 'We're doomed,' it said, 'we're clearly doomed, for having so offended thee!'

And he, because he could not see, simply grinned and squealed with glee:

'Yes, it seems you're likely doomed, I cannot say for sure. But it sounds like doom and it looks like doom, so yes, I'd say you're all quite doomed!'

Mere subterfuge. It changed nothing. He curled up into the fetal position on the bed.

Distractions, he thought, *infinite distractions, without which everything would be the same, except without distractions. And besides, I'm living in a foreign land.*

When Juan first considered applying to the university, he didn't think he'd actually be admitted. His GPA in high school was above average and he'd beefed up his college application with extracurricular activities—junior editor for the school newspaper and varsity track team. But the high school academic counselor, Dr. Westfield, a well-respected, elderly white man with a doctorate in education, suggested that he explore other options.

"You won't meet the academic standards of a four-year university," he'd advised. "Perhaps you should try getting into the local junior college or a good trade school."

So, upon the good doctor's advice, Juan reconsidered, even though he'd already filled out the university application and sealed it up in an envelope, postage stamp, and all. He didn't mail it, but kept it pinned to a cork board in his bedroom for several weeks. During that time, he considered his options; thought about attending the local community college in the fall, an educational institution, which its own students mockingly referred to as "Harvard on the Hill."

He also entertained the idea of joining the United States Army, like his older brother Richard had done after graduating from high school. A recruiting sergeant named Henry Canton had shown up one day for gym class; hoping to lure as many young boys as possible with the promise of decent pay, travel, and valuable trade skills. Juan had shown some interest; and so Sergeant Canton pulled him aside.

"The United States Army will provide you with what you need to make it in this world," he claimed.

Juan had told the sergeant that his big brother had enlisted, had gone to Jump School and served as a paratrooper.

"Your brother is a smart man," he replied with delight. "Did he tell you the Army offers the best training a young man could get in life? The U.S. soldier is the modern-day Spartan. That's a fact, you can look it up. Did your brother tell you that every penny you earn is yours to spend, because the Army provides you with housing and three square meals a day? And you won't have to pay for clothes because you'll be given a stipend to pay for uniforms. Did he happen to mention the many U.S. military bases throughout the world, so you might be stationed in Germany, Okinawa, maybe even Hawaii? Oh, and by the way, women love a man in a uniform. How's that sound, Juan?"

It appealed to him, to his sense of worth. The United States Army would accept him; he need not worry about not qualifying. The next day he took a bus to the recruiter's office, where he was greeted by Sergeant Canton with a big congenial grin and a firm hand shake. He was offered tepid, black coffee, stale donuts and a comfortable folding chair.

"I'm glad you decided to join the team," said Sergeant Canton. "That's a good man. You're making the right choice here, Juan."

The sergeant reached into a file cabinet, drew out a contract and placed it on the table with a ballpoint pen.

Juan hesitated. He wasn't ready to sign up just yet. He needed reassurances. He was thinking about the university application dangling on the cork board on his bedroom wall.

"Well, are you ready to sign up?" asked Sergeant Canton. "Are you ready to make the best decision of your life?"

"I was thinking about going to college," he admitted.

The sergeant had given him a smug grin, while slyly sliding the contract closer to Juan.

"College? That would be a waste of time for a young man like you. You need to experience life first hand, travel the world,

10

like your brother. And besides, what's the cost to go to college nowadays? Thirty, forty grand? Hell, you're going to have a hard time getting financial aid. That's a fact. You have to be filthy rich or dirt poor to go to college these days."

Sergeant Canton sipped his coffee, picked up the ballpoint pen and clicked it open.

"The Army will offer you a G.I. Bill; that's thirty thousand dollars in your pocket. All you have to do is enlist for four years. Then, once you've served, you can use the money to go to college. How's that sound?"

Juan said nothing; and the sergeant—sensing that the sales pitch hadn't worked, had offered him more tepid black coffee and stale donuts—suggested that he view a film about life in the Army, to which he reluctantly agreed.

In a dimly lit back room, Juan took a seat on a cold, metal folding chair. Sergeant Canton pushed play on the DVD player and the film began.

On a small, color TV set, a U.S. Army officer appeared and introduced himself as Captain Hayes, then proceeded to praise the particular military branch to which he belonged. He spoke the words Sergeant Canton had spoken almost verbatim. All the while, Juan sipped tepid, black coffee and took note.

After a few minutes, Juan was watching stock footage of soldiers marching double-time through dark woods in full battle gear, M1 Abrams tanks rolling in combat formation across a desert landscape, leaving dust clouds in their wake—the armored cavalry, a voiceover called them, Spearhead, Old Ironsides and Hell on Wheels; and a clip of gun-ho Airborne Rangers leaping head first out of the back of a C-130 Hercules.

The film ended with a catchy, patriotic sounding song and the image of the American flag flapping vigorously in the wind. Sergeant Canton walked into the room, smiling optimistically.

"Well, what'd you think Juan," asked the sergeant. "Did you like what you saw?"

Juan hadn't answered right away. He sat there stalling for time, thinking, and finally said:

"I want to think about it some more. I'm not ready to sign up just yet."

In reality, he was remembering how his mother had cried all night when his brother Richard left for basic training. He remembered how much the recruiting sergeant who had come for his brother had sounded like a used car salesman, having promised that he'd be stationed in Frankfurt, Germany, when he had actually ended up in Fort Benning, Georgia. And though his brother had few regrets, Juan knew in his heart that it'd be a mistake for him to enlist. He thought about what he really wanted, a college education, thanked the sergeant for his time and promptly walked out of the U.S. Army recruitment office.

The next day, disregarding all of the sound advice he'd gotten from Dr. Westfield and Sergeant Canton, Juan mailed the university application.

He waited patiently, and six weeks later received a large, bulky envelope in the mail. He opened it and read the cover letter inside:

"Dear Juan, congratulations! You have been accepted to the University of Los Angeles, California (ULAC) for the fall semester . . ."

He hadn't read any further. He just sat there with an

irrepressible smile on his face, clutching the admissions letter in his hand, as if it were the winning lottery ticket, muttering:

"I'm going to college . . ."

In the morning, gray sunlight glowed dim through the dusty transom of his dorm-room and roused him. It was an unusually cold, Southern California morning. That, and the fact that he had only gotten a few hours of sleep, made it extremely hard for him to get out of bed. Bundled fetal-like in a blood-red sarape, he rolled onto his side and sank back to sleep. But soon the sound of his own snoring startled him. Slow and somnolent, he sat up in bed, wiped drool from his cheek.

Chadwick Hall was silent now and cold. Cloaked in the sarape, he shivered, breathing in slow, quick gasps of air. He saw his own breath and it worried him, because he had been born with a pulmonary condition and was extremely susceptible to inclement weather. It was raining and the raindrops, blown askew by the wind, tapped on the transom. Cars sped out of the dormitory hall parking lot, casting distorted, specter-like silhouettes. Tires treaded eerily across the wet asphalt and splashed the transom. He was sitting, in fact, below the parking lot, because his dorm-room was an underground basement dormitory. A cold and damp subterranean cave.

He sat in bed until his eyes adjusted to the morning light, until his lungs breathed in enough oxygen to stimulate his brain. Only then, when it was impossible to hit the snooze button on his circadian clock, did he rise to his feet.

The first lecture of the day would begin promptly at eight a.m. and it was now half past seven. He shuffled barefoot across the concrete floor to the closet, where his clothes hung neatly on wire hangers. His clothes were not new, but were in good condition. He inspected every article of clothing carefully, checking for missing buttons and ironing out small wrinkles with the palm of his hand, picking lint from the shirt collar. Satisfied, he cast aside the scarlet serape and started to dress in front of the mirror.

He pulled a clean, white undershirt over his rather large head, slipped on khaki pants and a black and white flannel shirt. Then slowly, and quite deliberately, he began buttoning the flannel shirt from the bottom up. He always made a conscious effort to start at the bottom and work his way up. Once, and only once, he inadvertently started buttoning from the top and, catching an accidental glimpse of himself in the mirror, noticed how much he resembled one of those young, Mexican-American hoodlums in the barrio—a shaved head, gang affiliation tattooed on the forearms and on the neck, and attire to match, dark sunglasses, oversized Dickie pants, a white T-shirt and a Pendleton plaid shirt with only the top button buttoned.

Juan remembered thinking, *I look like a pinche cholo!*

That wasn't him, but to a good number of the residents living in Chadwick Hall he may as well have been one, judging by the way they nervously avoided making eye contact with him whenever he walked passed them in the lobby of the hall or on campus.

He wondered what they saw, wondered if he was really so very terrible to look at and, as he finished dressing, turned quickly to face himself again in the mirror, imagining that he was seeing himself for the very first time. There was this tall, thin, young man in his early twenties, a head too big for the body, a Mexican Indian

14

head, a full head of coarse black hair, a dark, broad face with large, solemn eyes and, standing in profile, an aquiline nose. He ran a fingertip along the curvature of the bridge, musing:

Look at that big, hideous Griffin beak, as big as my father's nose, bigger, throw that nose into the Los Angeles River and it wouldn't sink. The bridge would span the river.

Having seen too much, he looked away.

Plopping down on the bed, he put on two pairs of thick, gray, wool socks. From beneath the bed he pulled a second-hand pair of black, leather jump boots and set them on his lap. These had been handed down to him by his older brother Richard, the ex-United States Army paratrooper. The laces were threadbare and knotted, but the boots themselves were polished to a spit shine. The sole stitching along the arch of the left boot, however, was coming undone. He examined it at length, like a cobbler, and finally snatched up a copy of the Daily Kodiak, the university newspaper, from a dusty stack at the foot of the bed. He intended to make a patch to fix the hole in the boot, but an advertisement on the back page distracted him, a shoe sale at a local Village footwear shop. The ad showed a dozen types of shoes, but one pair in particular caught his attention.

"Men's leather tennis shoes," he read. "Lightweight, cushioned sole, only $99.99."

Staring intently at the picture of the stylish, white tennis shoes, he reasoned with himself until the desire to have the shoes left him.

"You don't even play tennis, *pendejo*," he said. "It's *their* sport. You wouldn't feel comfortable in those shoes. Read the shoe tag. It always tells the truth—'White man made upper sole, synthetic sock, made in America'. No, you wouldn't feel comfortable in those shoes."

Tearing out the page with the shoe advertisement on it, he quickly folded it into a crude patch and tucked it into the left boot. He shifted it from side to side and smiled, satisfied with his handy-work. He put on his jump boots as the bells of Farrington's Obelisk, audible from clear across campus in the crisp morning air, struck a quarter of eight.

"*¡Vámonos a la chingada!*" he said.

He prided himself on being punctual, and wasting no time now rushed out. In his absence, the dorm-room went completely silent, except of course for the constant tapping of raindrops against the transom window. It seemed to be coming down harder now, as if the rain knew that he had left the relatively safe shelter of Chadwick Hall.

2

There was a broad, herringbone, redbrick footpath that wound a quarter of a mile to the heart of the campus, with barren maple trees and Lombardy poplars growing on either side of it. Wet foliage lay strewn everywhere, making the path slippery. Juan moved along hurriedly, cautiously, his head lowered to shield against the sting of raindrops and what he perceived to be unfriendly looks from some of the students walking in the opposite direction. Off to the left was the intramural sports field, where fraternity brothers muddied themselves playing football on cold, autumn mornings, and to the right was the Ansgot Sports Pavilion, which resembled an inverted, salt-white ziggurat and was home to the Kodiak basketball team.

Juan pressed on, across the main square, greeted in passing the lone statue of Doctor Woolsey, the university's founding father—a tall, stolid-faced, spectacled gentleman whose fine, three-pieced tailored suit had been sullied by pigeon droppings. Doctor Woolsey did not return the salutation. A self-proclaimed man of vision, his gaze was perpetually upturned to the sky, to the heavens. Juan addressed the good doctor just the same, waved hello every morning, and at times had cordial words to say, *"¿Qué pasa, Woolys?"* or something to this effect. Today Juan simply nodded and, admiring the doctor's fashionable, wing-tipped, Oxford shoes, remarked:

"Hand-made by an Italian cobbler. Shoes fit for a king or a provost."

Up ahead, students sought shelter from the downpour in the Kodiak's Den, the university coffee house in the Student Union. He continued along the footpath as it twisted up a grassy, Norwegian pine-covered slope, where sickly-looking gray squirrels foraged for food. They looked harmless enough, but he kept his distance, remembering the warnings of the academic counselor during the freshman orientation campus tour.

"Never feed the squirrels," he was told. "They're very aggressive and quite possibly rabid."

Never feed the squirrels, he thought, his stomach grumbling. *As if I could afford to.*

Half way up the wooded slope the path diverged. The red brick footpath stretched on for another hundred yards or so in the direction of the grand Northern Quad. He turned off short of the quad, onto a narrow, asphalt trail, towards Lindsey Hall, all the while glancing over his shoulder to make sure that the squirrels hadn't followed him.

Lindsey Hall, like so many of the university buildings, had been designed in the Romanesque style, as if to suggest the rich academic tradition of the Renaissance. Juan thought that it was one of the grandest buildings on campus. Whenever he saw it, he was moved to a sense of awe, pride and affinity, because to him it epitomized the university, an institution older and more illustrious than anything that he had ever belonged to in his life. But the feeling quickly went away as he approached the hall, as the row of fantastic, reptilian gargoyles guarding the doors leered down at him, spewed rainwater and sneered as he went lumbering up the

18

low steps. If they meant to scare him off, however, to protect the hall, they had failed miserably. It would have taken much more than cold water and ugly glares from the heights of the parapet. Perhaps nothing short of a deluge of hot blood spouting from their gaping, stony mouths. He waltzed right in, quietly reciting *Beowulf*.

"The creature deprived of joy came walking to the hall. Quickly the door gave way, fastened with fire-forged bands, when he touched it with his hands. After that the foe at once stepped onto the shining floor, advanced angrily. He saw many men in the hall, a band of kinsmen."

And after Juan had stepped foot inside of the hall, thinking: *Not my kinsmen.*

The lecture hall was a large, fan-shaped arena that could seat up to three hundred students, but it was half empty today due to the bad weather. From the safety of the vestibule, he watched students drinking coffee, perusing the Daily Kodiak and looking over last week's study notes, waiting for Professor Kennington to arrive.

After surveying the room and determining that it was safe, he went dripping down the steps, carefully avoiding eye contact with the other students. He wouldn't look at them, not directly anyhow, and then only if they were not looking at him. He sat in the first unoccupied seat, a left-handed, tablet arm chair, and settled in for the two-hour lecture. There was time yet to catch up on his reading. From the inside of his coat he pulled the *Norton Anthology of English Literature*, a massive book with twice as many pages as the Holy Bible and a likeness of Queen Elizabeth the First on the dust jacket—the shrewd old matriarch of the kingdom, the Virgin

Queen standing steadfast and obstinate on the map of her beloved England, dressed in a magnificent, jewel-studded gown, looking pale and grim. She looked deathly ill to him, like death itself.

Opening the anthology to the dog-eared page, he read to himself.

Several rows back, a couple of students were talking about a party they had gone to the night before. And try as he did to focus on the text, their voices interfered, imposing themselves on his consciousness. He was forced to re-read the same lines, drawing absolutely no meaning.

"Then his heart laughed, dreadful monster. He thought that before the day came he would divide the life from the body of every one of them,"

Oh, my God he was so wasted! He blacked out in the kitchen. Scott and Josh had to carry his ass out to the car, but he came to and he was like 'I'm okay, I can walk,' and Josh was like 'Dude, I don't think so. You drank a fifth of Jack.'

"Then his heart laughed, dreadful monster . . ."

I was talking to Kim—Kim who—Kim Whitfield, she invited me to her parents' vacation home in Kauai for Spring Break—where in Kauai—Hanalei Bay—Oh, Jonathan's parents own a house in Hanalei Bay, it's awesome. I spent a few weeks there, last summer.

"He thought that before the day came . . ."

So the campus police showed up around one in the morning and asked us to, please, keep it down.

"He would divide the life from the body of every one of them."

The voices suddenly fell silent, as Professor Kennington had finally arrived. He walked in through a narrow side door with a subtle nod of his head as a greeting and an acknowledgment of his tardiness. He was a short, frail, silver-haired old gentleman in his late seventies who had been teaching English literature for over fifty years. He had retired the year before last and, in recognition of distinguished service to the university, had been conferred with Emeritus Status. But the university chancellor had seen fit to woo him back with adulation and a sizable bonus to instruct a course on Old English literature.

Professor Kennington moved cautiously toward the lectern, clutching in his small, sun-blotched, arthritic hand an ancient, black leather briefcase. Laying it gently on the lectern, he opened it and took out a bundle of crinkled lecture notes on index cards, yellowed with age, bound with a brittle rubber band. With trembling hands, he eased the briefcase shut and set it at his feet. For a moment he stood absolutely silent, looking ancient in his old, gray, tweed suit, gazing absent-mindedly at nothing in particular, as if he could not recall what he intended to say, as if he had completely forgotten who or where he was. Then he blinked and was present again. He reached into his coat pocket, produced a pair of horn-rimmed eye-glasses and put them on his wrinkled face. Hands unsteady, he held the lecture notes up to the light, fumbling them, squinting to decipher smudged words and illegible sentences. When he was ready to begin, he reclined against the lectern for support. His voice had lost its vigor from the decades of lecturing. These days he used a microphone. Clearing the phlegm from his throat, he stammered and spoke.

"Good morning. Today we will discuss . . ."

He wheezed and coughed.

"*Beowulf* . . ."

He coughed and wheezed.

"*Beowulf*," he continued, "is the oldest epic poem written in the English language. It was composed in the late tenth century by an unknown author, who most scholars, including myself, believe was a native of the West Midlands of England. The original manuscript was kept in London, along with the rare collection of medieval English manuscripts amassed by Sir Robert Bruce Cotton."

Juan scribbled frantically, trying to record every word Professor Kennington said.

"Unfortunately, in 1731, before a modern transcription could be made, the manuscript was badly damaged in a fire and many of the poem's lines were lost."

Here Professor Kennington paused for a moment and lowered his head, as if to contemplate and lament the loss.

"And yet," he continued, "despite this tragedy, the manuscript maintained its unique splendor, in both tone and style, and by virtue of its antiquity, and due to the fact that it is the first major poem written in a European vernacular language, *Beowulf* indeed merits a permanent place in the English literary canon."

Juan filled a notebook page, turned to a blank page, and shook his ballpoint pen so that the ink would flow evenly. Meanwhile, Professor Kennington rambled on.

"It tells of two Scandinavian tribes, ancient warrior societies who valued courage and vengeance, as opposed to the Christian doctrines of humility and mercy."

This last bit of information captivated Juan's imagination, causing the synapses in his brain to fire like pistons, explode like skyrockets.

Beowulf, he mused, *is a heathen.*

Juan stopped taking notes and began sketching a likeness of the pagan hero. He drew a long, hard face with a prominent brow, a narrow nose and savage blue eyes. On the strong, square chin he penned an unkempt beard, and on the head wild, greasy locks and a high Viking helmet with long, exaggerated ox horns and cheek-guards carved with images of ferocious boars. When he had finished the sketch, he stared at it a long time, nodding his head as if identifying a suspect in a composite drawing. Below the picture he scribbled the caption:

Beowulf the Barbarian.

"Our hero," said Professor Kennington, "is Beowulf, or Beow, as most scholars now agree his name should read. He is an archetype . . ."

Juan tried to concentrate on the lecture, but his mind wandered. Looking at the sketch, he grinned and scribbled the word: *Feo* in parenthesis below the caption. It made perfect sense to him and amused him so much that he laughed hysterically into the palm of his hand. He turned to see if anyone had seen him laugh, but they were oblivious to his glee.

Not funny, he thought, *because to them Beowulf is beautiful. He is their hero.*

They listened half-heartedly to the lecture. Some, like a student in the third row, slept through it all. A teaching assistant sitting in the front row yawned incessantly, unabashedly. Professor Kennington, meanwhile, was oblivious to his own sleep inducing discourse. He had paused a moment to fumble with the stack of index cards. Reaching into his coat pocket, he groped for something which wasn't there. Visibly irritated, mouthing silent curses, he rummaged in another coat pocket, from which he eventually pulled, like a senile magician, a white handkerchief. He blew his nose and the noise, amplified by the microphone, sounded like an agitated elephant. Cramming the handkerchief back into his coat pocket, he sorted the index cards.

Professor Kennington yawned, his small mouth stretched wide, exposing tea-stained dentures above gray gums.

"Excuse me," he said. "Where was I? Oh, yes, Grendel, known as the Rover of Borders, the Terrible Walker Alone, comes to Heorot Hall, not knowing that *Wyrd* demands his demise."

The other students nodded their heads knowingly, while Juan shifted his skinny haunches in the damp seat, suddenly sitting erect and at attention, but still befuddled, wondering:

What the fuck is Weird?

"*Wyrd*, as you all know," said Professor Kennington "is the guiding principle of Heathenry. It is the belief that all outcomes of all past deeds settle in the *Well of Wyrd*, where they sit and eventually emanate as the source of all of the outcomes of all future deeds. However, nothing is fixed. No event is set in the Loom of Time. Therefore, the face of things to come can be altered by the outcomes of new deeds, which are constantly flowing into the *Well of Wyrd*."

He started to write down every word Professor Kennington had said, but became confused by the meaning and wrote:

Weird is the Anglo-Saxon belief that everything that they do or do not do, be it good or bad, fills up the Well of Weird. And everything that they have done and have not done affects what will happen next. But nothing has been determined. Things can change.

"Stated succinctly," said Professor Kennington, "*Wyrd* is like

24

the German saying: *Sie sind deine Werke. You are your deeds.* Thus, when Beowulf boasts that he will slay Grendel, he is actually invoking *Wyrd*, as one would invoke God, asking it to recall his past deeds of manly courage and all of his shining victories, imploring *Wyrd* to bring about an equivalent outcome when he battles God's own enemy."

Juan had stopped writing now, doubting the sincerity of the lecture, thinking:

Beowulf's boasting isn't communion with Weird. It's pure vanity. A peculiar characteristic prevalent in these people. Professor K., too, pedantic old fart!

"Then there is Grendel," said the professor.

He wheezed, coughed and spat into his handkerchief, then continued, not using notes now, seemingly having committed this part of the lecture to memory, sharing it like a universal truth.

"According to the text, Grendel has no father. It tells us that he was begotten by dark spirits and that God does not love him."

Why doesn't God love him? Juan wondered.

"God does not love him," said Professor Kennington, "because he was condemned as Kin of Cain. He is an abomination. He belongs to the Loathsome Race."

Juan was keenly aware of how Professor Kennington's gaze wandered slowly and aimlessly across the sea of faces in the lecture hall, and how he spoke in monotone. And so he found it unusual that the professor had emphasized the words *loathsome race* and that his gaze had seemingly singled him out of the crowd, fixing itself on him when he uttered the words. It made him uneasy.

"And because he is an outcast," said the professor, "Grendel's deeds do not flow into the *Well of Wyrd*. His deeds are lost in the

Void. Nothing comes of them. It's as if he does not exist."

So, Juan concluded, *even if Grendel woke up one fine morning, cold, wet and miserable in his dark cave, and decided to be good, decided to stop gobbling up little white thanes, it wouldn't make a difference. The Loathsome Race is damned and so pobre Grendel is damned.*

A dark, unsettling, yet inexplicable sense of doom had come over him. He was conscious of being seated in Lindsey Hall, cognizant of the driveling academic standing at the lectern and of the assembly of detached classmates amongst whom he sat. And yet, he knew that he was not actually in the lecture hall, not occupying the seat in which he sat. He did not exist.

He stopped listening to Professor Kennington. Gallows-grim, he lowered his head, understanding how serious the situation was, realizing the implications, yet not really knowing exactly what would happen next.

3

The day ended for Juan like so many other days: a slow, straggling march back to the dorms, as the world turning ushered in the dusk. Weakened by hunger and inauspicious news, he ascended Spangler Hill in the rain, in what resembled a retreat after a lost campaign.

"Good news comes late, if it comes at all," he said, looking up at the storm clouds. "Bad news is always right on time."

Coming out of the downpour, into the lobby of Chadwick Hall, he ran his wet boots along the plush red carpet and sniffed the air like a ravenous dog. The rich aromas originated in the hall's kitchen and tempted him so much that he followed his nose to the source. He moved slowly passed the line of students filing into the dining area, drawing scowls and suspicious, sidelong glances. But in his single-mindedness, he was blind to their stares. He could only smell ingredients and think solely of dishes.

Roast beef fillet, he thought, *rolled and fatted roasted beef fillet with crushed black peppercorns, American baked beans, smoked bacon and caramelized onions, white beans and black molasses, herb roasted chicken, bay leaf, thyme and basil, barley pilaf and olive rosemary bread, pan fried shad with shallots and oil roasted haricots, hot Mary cakes and . . .*

He sniffed the air.

And soup, he thought, *cream of fennel soup.*

He owed his discerning sense of smell and his keen, if limited knowledge of cuisine to his custom of sitting in the lobby

27

at meal times, to his habit of thumbing through cook books, and fine dining magazines in Perkins Library. But he hadn't actually tasted any of the food that he smelled or read about. These days he ate poorly. The student loans that he received helped him pay his tuition and allowed him to rent the basement dorm-room, the least expensive housing the university had to offer. And his part time job stocking shelves at the campus bookstore earned him enough money to buy textbooks and some provisions, but he could not afford the thousand dollars a semester for dining privileges in the dining hall. There were days, however, when he managed to sneak into the cafeteria undetected. Casually, trying not to seem obvious about it, he looked to see who was working the monitor station on this particular evening. A big, blond, oafish student sat vigilantly at the post, taking plastic meal cards from the hall residents and sliding them one by one through a scanner, deducting one meal credit. He looked like the type who took his job too seriously, perhaps a bitter, non-scholarship football player who had to work his way through college. He looked like he would oust, by the belt loop and shirt collar, any poor starving student who even tried to slip into the dining room under his watch.

I wouldn't if I were you, a voice inside of his head cautioned.

Turning about-face, he made his way to the stairwell door and descended, still haunted by the scent of something sweet.

Once underground, Juan skulked along the narrow, dimly lit passageway, as water and human waste flowed in the pipes overhead in a ghostly gush. Coming to his dorm-room, he unlocked the heavy, fire-rated door and shuffled inside. The door, set on spring hinges, shut automatically behind him. He hadn't left the banker's lamp on, and so the room was as dark as a cave. Yet he did not turn on the light. In the darkness, he was invisible and he felt safe. He'd been living here for nearly five years now and had long since measured and memorized its exact dimensions, knew the boundaries by heart and so needed no light.

In the center of the dorm-room, he slipped off his boots, his dank socks, and quietly undressed. He stood naked, pensive, thinking about nothing in particular. He was not thinking about his empty stomach, although it felt as if intestinal parasites were eating him alive. He hardly flinched when car headlights flashed through the transom window, momentarily blinding him and exposing him. It was only a sudden and unexpected memory of his father that startled him. As a boy his father had planted in Juan's mind a neurotic fear of catching pneumonia. It had stayed with him over the years and rose up like a herald of certain death if he ever went so much as few seconds without a shirt on his back.

"*Perdóname, Papá,*" he said. "*Sí, tienes razón, la pulmonía es la muerte.*"

Dutifully, he pulled on the blood red sarape and a pair of leather huaraches. Then, knowing exactly what his father expected of him, and not wanting to disappoint him, he went straight to the bureau at the foot of the bed and began rummaging through the top drawer. He drew out a neatly folded bath towel, an undershirt and underwear that smelled of lemon laundry detergent, and a plastic Ziploc bag that contained toiletries: a bar of soap, a toothbrush, a small tube of toothpaste, a rusty shaving razor and a black plastic comb.

Out in the passageway, he skulked along again, passed the silent stairwell and the darkened laundry room, to the lavatory.

It was not a spacious bathroom, not like the ones up above. This one, with walls so close that it seemed to have been built not to provide privacy, but to confine, had only one toilet, one sink and, within that already limited space, a single shower stall.

Facilities meant to accommodate a single man, he mused. *And whosoever lives in dorm-room B-111 is that man. I am that man.*

He disrobed, set his belongings on a little wooden bench and, with the sage-scented soap in hand, parted the heavy, plastic shower curtain and stepped trembling into the shower stall. Turning on the hot water knob, he immersed his body in the steaming spate of water. It was hardly bearable, but he endured it, on his head, his hands, and on his back. Palming the soap, he moved it in slow circles on his hairless chest, working his way down to his ribs and abdomen. Spumes purled down his shins and eddied in the drain. He soaped his navel, while staring sadly at the shriveled, brown appendage dangling between his thighs.

Poor little monkey, he thought. *I haven't touched it in months, not since I saw that gorgeous, big breasted Salvadorian woman on the bus. God she was something! She had everything a woman needs to birth a million beautiful, brown babies. We could people the world anew after the polar caps melt and drown mankind.*

Under the pretense of being thorough and clean, he soaped it, stroked it awhile, allowing himself a little pleasure, but eventually lost interest.

With renewed purpose and vigor, he scrubbed his knees, calves and ankles. He scrubbed away dead skin and live skin alike, all the while whispering something. He was debating with himself, nodding and shaking his head, affirming and negating opposing points of view in turn. In the end he smiled, seemingly coming to

30

an agreement, acknowledging truth on the subject.

"Yes," he bellowed, "the man who has bathed has no need to wash. A good choice of words if you happen to be a savior. A poor choice of words if you're a soap salesman. The man who has bathed has no need to wash, except for his feet. Yes, but *I* wash my own feet."

He washed his feet and proceeded to comb his frothy fingers through his hair, forming a sudsy white cap atop his head. As he did this, lather trickled into his eye.

"Christ!" he screamed.

He thrust his face under the showerhead to flush out the sting, stuck a knuckle into his tear-duct and grit his teeth. The pain of lye soap in his eye soon washed away, but thoughts of the day, of Kennington's prophecy, stayed with him. It would not wash out of his head. He turned off the hot water knob and stood there in silence for a while, in the dense, warm mist of scalding water, in the stillness left behind by the cessation of falling water. He could hear a faint, but familiar voice calling out to him by name, refuting the professor's prophecy. Curious, he jerked his head back, like a baby responding to the sound of its father's voice. He recognized it, was drawn to it and comforted by it, and though he did not know what the words meant, and lacked the language to respond, he understood it intuitively.

"Yes," he finally said, finding a bit of solace in it. "Good things will come, if you can only survive the bad things."

Parting the heavy, plastic shower curtain, which now resembled a delicate white veil, he stepped out of the stall. After drying his body, he got dressed, pulled on the blood red sarape, slipped on his huaraches, collected his things and exited the bathroom. As he returned to his dorm-room, down the dim passageway, he shone by a light of his own creation, his face aglow.

Not having eaten anything since noon—a stale, savorless sandwich and tepid black coffee, purchased from vending machines on campus—he sat at the table and got ready to prepare a late night meal. The middle drawer served as a makeshift pantry and having opened it, he stared into it for a very long time, gazed expressionless at what it did or did not contain. There wasn't much: a half of a loaf of white bread, a tin of anchovies, and a small ration of butter, a dish and a knife (the last three items having been pilfered from the hall's cafeteria); he arranged them neatly on the little table, by the light of the banker's lamp.

He made a buttered fillet of anchovy sandwich, quartered it, blessed it and ate.

Chew, he mused, *mouth to the stomach, down to the J-shaped stomach, to that dark digestive hole. Churn, stomach to the rectum, food particles miraculously imbibed into the walls of the small intestine, small, medium or large intestines, and into the blood stream to nourish the body. A miracle, and then gas.*

He belched and bellowed:

"And because *He* was without anything to eat *He* fed himself."

When he had eaten his fill, he wrapped up the leftovers, enough to feed a thousand starving students, and stored them in the middle drawer. Using the back of his hand as a napkin, he wiped anchovy oil and breadcrumbs from his lips.

In the morning, early morning, he would rise and bathe and eat again. He would march dutifully to Perkins Library to read his books and end the day much like this day.

"To bed," he said, like a mandate he needn't have made to his spent body. "To bed."

4

Juan smelled rain. Despite the prospect of good weather, marked by broken bands of blue sky and fleeting rays of sunlight, he smelled rain. He was walking along the redbrick footpath again, not looking at the path at all. He surveyed the sky, watched the cumulus clouds drifting inland, shifting shape and color, merging, mounting and going from salt white to silver, dark violet to black. A drop fell on his nose, followed by a thousand drops dotting the dry brick path. Then it fell hard and it thundered and he started running, sought shelter because, among other things, he feared electrical storms.

The first building that he came to was Kaplan Hall, the university psychology building. It was said that Doctor Woolsey had personally handpicked the architects who designed and built the hall, back in the late 1950s, the best young minds from the firm of Wikowski, Linderman and Gold out of New York City. It had been fashioned after what they'd imagined cities of the future to look like—a minimalist, flat-roofed, slab-shaped structure of metal, brick and glass. The original architectural drawings, set out in display cases in the lobby of Kaplan Hall, depicted the hall and the university as they might appear to future generations: glass research towers stretching sixty stories into the sunlit clouds, erected on perfectly symmetrical lawns, manicured by means of artificial intelligence, robotic gardeners designed by the school's very own mechanical engineers, fountains like geysers spurting crystal blue waters a thousand feet into the air, sprinkling the bellies of colossal, automated aero-ships, flying seminars cruising overhead. And rendered so masterfully in the drawings was the ethereal quality of light that constituted the day in this supposed utopian world.

Here was Juan now, on the high steps of Kaplan Hall, a half a century later, thinking how dated the whole thing looked. What's more, the building had a clinical feel to it and reminded him of a building in a different kind of institution altogether. Not venturing any further than the large, double glass doors, he peered inside and what he saw made him feel uneasy. There was a long, main entryway that led into a maze of narrow, faintly lit corridors, presumably leading into the innermost parts of the hall, into the depths of the university's encephalon. It made him think of the promise of psychology—'*to probe the deepest mysteries of the mind.*' A frightening thought.

Don't go in there, a voice warned him, even as the glass doors reflected the darkening sky and the ominous flash and glow of lightening overhead.

Juan backed away slowly, like the stray cats that roamed the university grounds, who were said to instinctually avoid the medical compounds on the northside of campus, fearing abduction by cold-blooded vivisectors.

Ducking into the adjoining building, the Student Union, he breathed a sigh of relief. The foyer was cozy and well lighted, furnished sparsely with vermilion colored sofas, end tables and gold shaded banker's lamps. Across the way he could see a row of brand new vending machines, candy bars and pastries, chips and cellophane wrapped sandwiches, shining by florescent light behind the glass. He was ravenous and in his pants' pocket jingled coins, which he had saved for laundry, but now intended to use to buy breakfast. But between him and morning nourishment sat a sickly-looking, blond co-ed in a gray, university sweatshirt, slumped uncomfortably in the corner of a sofa, blowing her rosy nose into a hard wad of tissue paper. She was short, pale and noticeably underweight, her countenance suggestive of something lifeless. Yet beyond her stark appearance, she had another quality about her, inborn and indefinable, that terrified Juan. Perhaps it was the particular shade of blue in her eyes or perhaps it was the angle at which she held the finite math book in her hands that seemed to imperil his life. He could not say for sure. But the fear was real and it was crippling.

After a moment she must have sensed Juan's presence, because she stopped reading and looked up at him, somewhat uneasily, through thick-lens glasses. He, meanwhile, was thinking of a way to get around her and to the vending machines.

Go to the kiosk, he thought, *but don't look at her. Go to the ATM machines, move fast, but stay calm. And don't look at her. Go to the telephones, but don't stop. Cut across the sitting area to the vending machines, but whatever you do don't look at her.*

Moving quickly, he skirted the sofas and followed the mental map that he'd laid out for himself to the vending machines. He made it. Knowing exactly what he wanted, he inserted three dollars' worth of quarters and made his selection. Three small, apple Danish fell into the open compartment below and he snatched them up and devoured them whole. They sat heavily in the pit of his stomach, like lumps of coal, and he knew very well that he would have trouble digesting them. It left him grimacing and clutching at his stomach, as if he had been poisoned. Then, quite unexpectedly, the pain went away. He looked back at the sofas, having inadvertently turned around, and noticed that the sickly-looking, blond co-ed had vanished. And the pain had gone too. Convinced that there was some correlation, his curious mind automatically attempted to connect the two occurrences.

Where did she go? Juan wondered. *She was sitting there just now. I turned and she was gone. Where did the pain go? It was with me just now. She went forth and with her went the pangs of hastily eaten pastries. Where did she go? Where did the pain go?*

Still wary, he walked to where she had been sitting, well aware that she might return at any given moment. There was a slight indentation in the sofa cushion and, moved by a sense of awe and self-preservation, he touched it, checked it for heat and found that the seat was cold. Satisfied that he was now alone, he sat in her stead, warmed the seat. He decided to sit there awhile, because the rain would not stop falling.

From between the sofa cushions, he rooted out a copy of yesterday's Daily Kodiak and leafed through it to pass the time. He read about the big basketball game played last night in the Ansgot Sports Pavilion and how the home team had defeated its cross-town rivals by a slim margin in the final seconds of the contest. News of the victory surprised him, elated him and made him feel that he had some part in the win simply because he happened to be a student attending this particular university. But when he began to question why it brought him so much happiness the feeling went away. It occurred to him that he had no special connection to the winning basketball team. He was not a fan of the sport. It wasn't his victory.

He read an advertisement offering summer employment in the Alaskan fishing industry, requiring no previous experience, only a willingness to work hard. The ad promised good pay and stipulated free room and board and air-travel to and from Alaska, so long as the employee fulfilled all contractual obligations. It appealed to him, the prospect of going north, the promise of what seemed like a good opportunity. Would it be worth it, he wondered, to travel so far north to work on a fishing trawler or in a cannery? Alaska is a big state, he reasoned, and a world away from home. What if he did go north and things got bleak and he got lost in the frozen wilderness? Seward's Folly becoming his own folly. Undecided, he circled the ad with a pen.

There was an announcement, printed by the University Crisis Intervention Center, offering mental health services to students experiencing loneliness, stress or depression, to students contemplating suicide, but he had hardly glanced at it when an article on the facing page diverted his attention. It read:

Colorado Students March to Protest Racist Flyers
By Mary Hill
The Associated Press
DENVER - Hispanic students congregated on the Centennial State College campus Tuesday to condemn racist flyers distributed sometime Monday night. The flyers, inserted into university newspapers, demanded that the United States government "build a wall, mine the borders, place bounties on 'wet backs' heads and send Mexicans back to their country in body bags." The group that

distributed the flyers called themselves *United Students Against the Brown Menace.*

"Basically, they're saying that they want to kill Mexican students," said Mario González, spokesman for the *Mexican-American Resistance Coalition-Heritage of Aztlán*, the Hispanic student group that organized the rally.

An estimated 600 students congregated to express outrage, as M.A.R.C.H.A. leaders called for action from university administrators, citing an increase in campus hostility aimed at Hispanic students caused, in large part, by the passing of Proposition 187 in California.

Should the voter-approved initiative be implemented, it would deny educational and health care services to illegal immigrants in the state of California.

"This is the backlash of Prop. 187," stated González. "This is how hate begins to take root."

The flyers stated that "low-life Mexicans are invading American society, polluting the cultural landscape. Along with low IQs they bring drugs, disease, crime, poverty and ignorance."

Olivia Fricke, president of Centennial State College, denounced the flyers as "racist drivel" and added: "We share your indignation," pledging a thorough investigation of the incident.

Centennial State College professor Jaime Soto advised Hispanic students to "forgive the enemy" and not allow anger and resentment to become hate and reverse racism.

"We must walk with pride and dignity on campus," he stated. "Let them all know that we are honorable people. Let them see who Mexicans truly are."

When he had finished reading the story, he read it again. The whole human race was crazy, he decided. Why else would people discriminate against other people? Why else would they hate one another? Why else would a thing like racism exist? If such a racist leaflet had been buried in the pages of the Daily Kodiak, he didn't intend on finding it. He tossed the newspaper onto the floor, as if it were excrement, and marched sullenly out of the Student Union, into the pouring rain.

Perkins Library sat solemnly and serenely in the grand Northern Quad, above the Norwegian pine-covered slope. It looked to him very much like a painting of an Italian cathedral he had once seen in a history book detailing life in northern Italy at the height of the Renaissance: an immense structure, with lofty square towers, ornate turrets, dense walls, a colonnaded portico and an apse at the eastern end.

The young scholar's cathedral, he thought. *The temple of bright-eyed optimists who actually believe that they can save this wonderful world and all of the miserable people in it by reading books and sharing ideas and knowledge.*

He had stopped to read, for the hundredth time, the writing carved into the stone lintel above the main entrance, words of hope attributed to an Englishman named Faraday:

Nothing is too wonderful to be true.

Yet given the inclement weather and the cynical news of the day, he inverted the phrase to suit his own pessimistic mood, mumbling as he crossed the threshold:

"Everything is too terrible to be true."

An hour earlier, a prim and dutiful librarian had come from behind the circulation counter to unlock the library doors and a throng of diligent young women and men, who had until that very

40

moment been waiting faithfully out in the rain, rushed in. By the time he got to Perkins Library, they had already been toiling away at their studies for quite some time, hunched over like Jesuit monks perusing cryptic tomes, lost in erudition. He shuffled passed the Reading Room, grimacing at the sight of them, as he appreciated the irony of it. He had come here to do just that, because it was required of him as an undergraduate student, because if he did not he would fail and be dismissed from the university. What made the moment all the more poignant, what made it painfully absurd, was the glass case by the elevators, displaying a rare collection of fifteenth century English manuscripts on loan from Cambridge University. They had been set out in plain view, a dozen or so folios; the parchment was noticeably brittle, but the ink surprisingly not faded, with gold leaf adoring every initial letter and luminous, colorfast illustrations blazing on every page. Yet he didn't see them as priceless volumes, amassed and safeguarded for posterity. He saw a bundle of old books, left behind by their owners, abandoned by dead scholars. It made him recall something from a Psalm about how the foolish passed away and how, likewise, wise men would die. With a subtle nod, he slipped inconspicuously into the stairwell.

Up on the sixth floor, behind the stacks that held volumes on quantum physics, and right beside a window with an unobstructed view of the grand Northern Quad, he found his favorite, private study carrel unoccupied. He set his belonging down—the *Norton Anthology of English Literature*, a spiral notebook and a blue fountain pen. But prior to study, he examined the placard on the wall, not preoccupying himself with the official words that warned:

NO SMOKING AREA—NO FOOD OR BEVERAGES IN THE LIBRARY—BOOKS WILL BE REMOVED DAILY FROM CARRELS—DO NOT LEAVE PERSONAL BELONGINGS UNATTENDED

Quite familiar with these ordinances, he looked instead to the graffiti in the margins of the placard. He checked it periodically, like a lobster trap, to see what crass, comical or witty remarks had been added since the last time he'd read it. Silently, he read:

I deserve success (you will fail). Jesus loves everyone (except Jews, Muslims, Hindus and Buddhists). I want to go to law school (you're too stupid and can't afford it). Bomb the Middle East (if it is possible, as much as depends on you, live peaceably with all men). Girls like me because I'm a nice guy and, oh yeah, because I have a king-sized penis! Golly, isn't college neat? (Go to hell).

There was much more written there, but he stopped reading because it was too much for him to mentally process. Remembering why he had come, he opened up the spiral notebook, held it up like a hymn booklet in the palm of his hand and read his lecture notes and personal annotations of days past out loud.

"Cynewulf, Anglo-Saxon poet, a Northumbrian or Mecian, wrote in the 8th or 9th century, numerous poems attributed to Cynewulf, four in *The Exeter Book* and *The Vercelli Book*."

An annoyed voice on the other side of the stacks shushed him, but he continued reading, louder than before.

"*The Vercelli Book*, Old English manuscript written in England before 1000 A.D., now in the possession of the chapter of Vercelli, North Italy, contains *The Dream of the Rood* and four poems by Cynewulf."

Again he was shushed, but he waved his hand, as if swatting at a pesky fly.

"*The Exeter Book*," he read, "Old English manuscript of poems, transcribed 940 A.D. and donated by Bishop Leofric to Exeter Cathedral, contains *The Wanderer* and, unlike many Mayan codices, miraculously survived the ruinous touch of time and man."

He yawned, shifted in the chair, and set aside the spiral notebook, deciding that his time would best be spent catching up on his reading assignments. Placing the anthology in front of him, he opened it to the frontispiece, a detailed drawing of a magnificent snow white swan gliding effortlessly upon a mirror lake, and began skimming through the onion skin pages: first the bookplate, his name stenciled neatly inside the ornate, *ex libris* box: JUAN JUÁREZ BITOL. Next the table of contents, the preface, acknowledgments and introduction, *Caedmon's Hymn*, *The Dream of the Rood*, *Beowulf*, and *The Wanderer*.

The Wanderer was a poem which he had read three times; once because it was included on the syllabus as required course reading, a second time because the language was beautiful, the diction terse and lyrical, making him feel something which he did not understand, and a third time because he finally realized that what he felt was an affinity with the lost hero of the poem, the loneliness of the exile. Starting in on it for the fourth time, he read only the text that he had underlined.

He who is alone often lives . . . to tread the tracks of exile . . . fully fixed is his fate . . .

In these verses he perceived some truth, and acknowledged it by nodding his head and whispering: "Yes, the tracks of exile."

He kept reading.

So spoke the earth walker . . . remembering hardships . . . there is now none among the living to whom I dare clearly express the thought of my heart . . . all delight has gone . . . all this earthly habitation shall be emptied.

"Yes, all earthly habitation emptied," he said, nodding emphatically. He wondered what it would be like if the world were to be emptied of its inhabitants, namely mankind.

What if the human species suddenly emptied out? he thought. *Not due to war, plague, flood or famine. What if it simply emptied out, like an ornamental vase brimming with dirt, suddenly turned upside down by the very hand that filled it?*

His thoughts aflutter, like moths drunk on lamplight, he gazed wistfully out of the window with the unobstructed view, at the gray sky above and the dismal quad below. He imagined walking out of Perkins Library into a bright and vacuous world. The sun was shining now, golden peels of orange-scented rays warming his brow, his cheeks, and his nose.

There were no students sitting on the benches and no bicycles on the bike racks and it made him feel very happy. Certain that he was alone, he walked leisurely down the wooded slope, strolled along the deserted college path, surveyed the silent buildings. There was Monk Hall, emerald shag of ivy, brown brick and mortar, red tiled roof, windows and doors forming a structure with vacant rooms. Then Stidolff Hall, also known as "The Rocket Shelter", which was rumored to have been built as a fallout shelter for faculty members at the height of the Cold War. It was cold and empty. Next came the Student Union, ironically devoid of students. There was the Ansgot Sports Pavilion, which had hosted a sold out basketball game on the previous night. Here he stopped, peered into the sports arena through an open doorway, saw the dark court and ten thousand empty seats.

"Hello? Is anybody here?" he called out, just for good measure, only to hear his own voice echo in the steel rafters.

To the main square he wandered, amazed, elated. He met up with the statue of Doctor Woolsey, still gazing skyward, once oblivious to mankind, now equally oblivious to the absence of mankind. Juan greeted him nonetheless, smiled up at the statue lovingly. Then, knowing that there was no one left to shun him, he sat quietly at its feet to sun himself.

It was only a sudden sensation of an unknown presence that brought him back to Perkins Library. Behind him, three plain, white, featureless faces in profile, like identical, cardboard cut outs, passed rapidly, in quick succession through the stacks, heads independent of bodies. He turned in time to see them vanish behind a column. They circled back, however, and reappeared by the stairwell door, only to dissipate again, like smoke into a ventilation duct. His first instinct was to go to where he had last seen them, find them, and speak to them bravely, like a Mexican Hamlet, demanding: "What do you want? Speak to me or go away!" But then a second, involuntary impulse moved him. Abandoning all of his belongings, he got to his feet and made a panicked dash through the stacks. He didn't know where he was going. He only knew, intuitively, that he had to get as far away as possible, perhaps reacting like a frightened native would have upon seeing a fleet of galleons anchored off the coast of his native land, upon the grim realization that the strange, white, bearded men coming ashore on row boats meant death.

On the northside of the sixth floor, he stopped momentarily to catch his breath and, seeing that he hadn't been followed, snuck into an empty bathroom and hid in a toilet stall. In there it was quiet and apparently safe, but nevertheless he thought it prudent to secure the stall latch and shore up the stall door by propping his feet against it.

They might storm the bathroom, he reasoned, *and push their way into the stall. I don't think they saw me, but if they do and they come I'll be ready.*

Sitting recumbently on the toilet, he waited, his heart beating so fast that he thought it would implode. Nobody came, and yet he waited. He counted the little holes in the acoustic tiles on the ceiling, but finding them to be as infinite as the stars soon abandoned the task. He flushed the toilet a dozen times, at regular intervals, to pass the time, and when they still had not come for him he started reading the graffiti on the wall.

Like a slow-moving movie camera, his eyes panned the narrow section of the wall, systematically reading everything in large print first and everything in small print last. There were assorted types of political propaganda and philosophical queries, limericks laden with expletives and a prayer for nourishment, presumably penned by a starving student, an unfinished mathematical equation and a life-like sketch of a beautiful, young couple copulating, several bold, but ultimately insignificant declarations of existence, simply stating: so-and-so was here, and a Sphinx-like riddle which he dared not read out loud, doubting his ability to answer it, fearing retribution at the hands of the white monsters skulking around the sixth story stacks.

The last thing that he read was an acronym. It had been

carved at the bottom of the stall door with a sharp object. He bent down to get a good look at it and traced the letters with his finger, the paint peeling and flaking. After staring at it for a long time, he read it out loud, enunciating every syllable like a child learning how to read:

"M-A-R-C-H-A!"

His voice, like a depth sounding, traveled down to the bottom of a sea of time until it hit upon a lost memory, and the newly found memory echoed.

The Mexican American Resistance Coalition-Heritage of Aztlán, he thought. *The student organization that protested the racist flyers at Centennial State College. The group of Chicano students who once took me in at this university and who put me out. Here is that memory still, perfectly preserved in my mind, like a fossilized egg. It'll stay with me and go only after I go.*

5

It was late October, he recalled, *and the mornings were especially cold that fall. There were thousands upon thousands of dead, windblown leaves coming down lightly from the maple trees on campus, fluttering as they fell, and I crushed them underfoot.*

Ah no, he recanted, *the thousands upon thousands of dead maple leaves were actually Monarch butterflies, fire bright, orange and alive, flying slowly and nimbly across campus, flying south to Mexico. And, as I remember it, I did not crush them underfoot, because it is the worst sort of luck to kill a butterfly, because butterflies are the Happy Dead, the souls of our dearly departed ancestors returning to see to it that all is well with the living.*

Juan remembered taking that brisk walk across campus to Finney Hall on that crisp autumn morning, a strong wind plucking the last of the fall leaves from the maples, as he tried desperately not to crush them underfoot.

He was taking a course on Mexican history at the time and, in his haste to make it on time to the lecture hall, he had arrived a half hour early. In the undisturbed silence of the empty lecture hall, in the time between his arrival and that of the second student, he skimmed the imposing, plum rose colored textbook, with the design of an Aztec calendar on the cover—the sixth edition of *A History of the Mexican People.* The first few pages showed photographs of Pre-Columbian figurines, beautiful, ceramic dancers with swollen thighs, fierce, obsidian

48

warriors brandishing studded clubs, a fat, jade baby sucking its thumb and a basalt priest kneeling, with upturned head and mouth agape, invoking the gods.

A cross section of that ancient civilization in miniature, he remembered thinking. Their tiny heads, no bigger than those of dolls, were in stark contrast to the colossal, Olmec head on the next page. It sat unevenly at the edge of a sunny, Central American jungle, a diminutive Mexican boy in customary, white cotton garments and dusty, leather huaraches, standing beside it, adding scale to the gigantic head.

He stared at the black and white snapshot for the longest time, seeing something in it that both attracted him and disgusted him. It may have been the familiar facial features, the pudgy lips, the protruding eyes, and the enormous nose. It may have been the immensity of the head, ten feet high and twenty tons (according to the caption) that intrigued him, and at the same time made him feel deep, self-conscious revulsion.

Big, ugly deformed thing, he thought. *Eclipses the sun itself.*

So fixated was he on the photograph that he didn't even notice the other student who had come into the lecture hall, who had nonchalantly, but quite deliberately chosen a seat in the row behind him. The student sat staring at the back of Juan's head, marveling at how big it was and how thick and black the hair on it was in comparison to his own light, sandy brown hair.

You're rich in Indian blood, the student almost said, right out loud. *Look at that impenetrable head of hair, as thick as a South American jungle.*

"Our ancestors were giants," the student finally said.

"Excuse me?" said Juan, startled by the voice, turning abruptly.

"The Olmec head," he explained. "The people who made it were giants."

He stared silently at the student sitting behind him, considering what he had said. Then, not wanting to appear impolite, he smiled, nodded and turned around, thinking:

If our ancestors were giants, the Spanish Conquistadors were gods.

Juan continued skimming through the textbook and, in the middle chapters, which delineated the Spanish invasion of Mexico, came across photographs of sixteenth-century Spanish articles of war and conquest: kettle hat helmets worn by infantry men, elaborate chamfrons made to fit Spanish war horses, a shiny, blood-stained halberd, a wheel-lock pistol, and a crossbow. Examining all of these things, he suddenly gasped and pushed the textbook away. He had seen too much, like the time he saw photos of Nazi death camps, the Buchenwald nightmare, emaciated bodies of Jewish men, women and children stacked like firewood in the icy mud. And then there was that photograph in another history book of lynched black men, dangling barefooted from Southern poplars, swaying lightly in the cool, summertime breeze, their faces bloodied by the hands of the mob, their necks twisted, elongated by the rope, by the noose. In the foreground of the snapshot, a proud white man was staring directly into the camera lens, pointing to the lifeless bodies as if to say, 'This is what happens to uppity niggers around here!'

The memory of the images still haunted him. Now here was more of the same, staring up at him from the glossy pages of the Mexican history book. It wasn't that he personally feared the photographs. Rather, it was a strange sort of belated anxiety and panic that had set in on him, knowing that this weaponry had been used against his own ancestors, agonized by the fact that he could do absolutely nothing about it now. As he sat there distraught, the student sitting behind him volunteered commentary.

"Can you picture the look on an Aztec Jaguar Knight's face as a mounted Spaniard came charging, swinging a halberd at his head?"

Extending his arm, palm held upward, he made a swift, hacking motion.

"*¡Huacatelas! Ya estuvo.* And the crossbow and the gun? Marvelous technological advancements? Nah. Crude mechanism of death, so barbaric that popes mandated that they not be used against Christian enemies, because killing a Christian is a sin, but it was perfectly okay to use them against Arabs and *indios*, right?"

It was all news to him, although none of it surprised him.

Weapons of mass destruction sanctioned by men of God, he thought. *A perfect paradox, but somehow oddly fitting.*

He closed the book, weary of the subject and hoping to discourage further commentary. But the student sitting behind him leaned forward and introduced himself.

"My name is Pepe Moreno," he said.

He studied Pepe's face for a moment, trying to read his disposition in the subtle rumples of his fair-skinned brow, in the flawless, olive irises of his eyes, like a seer divining truth in tealeaves. Finally, unable to come to a conclusion, he introduced himself, mumbled, "Juan Juárez Bitol."

51

And as they shook hands Juan thought:

His heart is pumping Spanish blood. Look at his white skin. Funny, his name is Moreno.

Promptly at nine o'clock Professor Galindo sauntered into the lecture hall, dressed in an oversized, pearl white suit with brass buttons. Squat and dark, a dumpy man with big, disproportioned hands, he looked more like a Mexican field hand than a tenured academic. But when he spoke, all misconceptions were dispelled. He was well-educated, an East Coast intellectual, who spoke English, French, and Spanish, although he rarely spoke Spanish and when he did, it was with an affected, Anglicized accent. It may have been because he had a Spanish surname and a dark complexion, and so Professor Galindo had been mistaken for a janitor once too often, and thus was given to ostentation to compensate for his feelings of inadequacy; as when he boasted of his credentials on the first day of the term.

"I was educated in the Ivy League," he had said. "Undergraduate studies at Brown University, graduate and doctorate work at the University of Pennsylvania. I have served as the head of the History Department at La Universidad Nacional Autónoma de México and recently was granted academic tenure at this fine, academic institution."

Professor Galindo was very proud of his tenure status, especially since he was one of only a few Hispanic faculty members teaching at the university. Years of marking the seasons not by changes in the weather, but by the continuous cycle of terms, of learning to cope with the grueling demands of collegiate politics, had earned him a permanent position. He had published several

52

scholarly articles and a book, had tolerated patronizing deans and subtle, sometimes unwitting, bigoted jibes from his fellow professors, and now had been endowed with a kind of scholar's immortality. But to many of his students, he had simply become a pompous, lackey academic, prompting one of them to have commented:

"Can you believe this *cabrón?* Trying to act white, telling us he went to Brown and UPenn. Brown, UPenn *qué la chingada*. He means a Mexican prison!"

Professor Galindo stepped to the lectern as if it were a pulpit and stared solemnly across the lecture room. He had cavernous nostrils that, from a distance, made it look as if he had a little black mustache.

"Good day," he said. "I'll spend most of the morning talking about the *Porfiriato*, which will include a slide presentation. There may be time for questions."

"Porfirio Díaz was a pimp," Pepe mumbled.

If Professor Galindo had heard the remark, he was either ignoring it or did not care to respond at that moment, because he began his lecture with unwavering fervor.

"Porfirio Díaz," he said, "the hero of Puebla, the savior of Mexico, ascended into the presidency in the year 1876 and was charged with the task of bringing social and economic stability to a country in shambles."

He proceeded to recount how Díaz set out to save Mexico from itself, expounding on the plan to attract foreign capital. Preparatory to anything, he explained, Díaz had to establish order or at the very least the semblance of it. This he achieved by military means. *Pax Mexicana*, he called it. With a kind of vicarious exuberance, he related how, within a few years of his first term, Díaz had been officially recognized by the majority of western European governments and, most importantly, by the United States. It was Porfirio Díaz, he maintained, who provided the impetus that vaulted Mexico into an era of modernization and prosperity. A great man, he mumbled.

Pepe was writhing in his seat, indignant, looking around at his classmates, wondering why they, too, were not outraged.

"Professor Galindo," he finally said. "Isn't it true that Porfirio Díaz fits the political definition of a tyrant?"

"No," said Professor Galindo, "not necessarily."

"Didn't he use the military to remain in power for over thirty years, while perpetuating an illusion of democracy? Didn't he shamelessly allow foreigners to exploit Mexico's natural resources? And didn't he dispose of political opponents and censor the press?"

"Perhaps, but it was for the common good of Mexico."

"What about the revolutionary slogan: *México para los Mexicanos.*"

"Porfirio Díaz *was* a Mexican," said the professor.

Professor Galindo was becoming exasperated with what he saw as an affront to his expertise.

"Mr. Moreno," he finally said, "if you'd like to continue this discussion please see me during my office hours. Now is not the time to debate the possible wrongdoings of the *Porfiriato*. We're here to study Mexican history, not to hang Díaz in effigy. He is a long time in the grave."

"A long time in hell," whispered Pepe.

"Okay," said Professor Galindo. "Let's continue. Porfirio Díaz, the savior of Mexico . . ."

Between Professor Galindo's lecture and the slide show, there was a short break, during which time a good number of the students left the room. A few dawdled in the hallway, made quick calls on their cell phones. Some of them went out for coffee and hot bagels. Others left and didn't come back. Juan stayed put and, at the moment, was watching a small group of his classmates through the frosty windows, whom were huddled in the square outside of Finney Hall, like a throng of lepers, smoking cigarettes.

Exciting new vice, he thought. *Chain-smoking college kids. No worries. Mom and dad far away. Lung cancer years away. I will go to med school, become a doctor, find a cure, and heal them as they lay dying. Sabes qué . . . chale!*

In the row behind him, he could hear Pepe diligently scouring through the middle pages of *A History of the Mexican People,* highlighting passages. He seemed intent on stock piling new information and knowledge, as a warring faction amasses arms and ammunition in preparation for an upcoming offensive. Apparently he hadn't been deterred by the tongue-lashing he'd been given and was now planning a second challenge to Professor Galindo's authority on the subject of Mexican history.

Juan listened to the flutter of turning pages and thought of the pigeons in Hollenbeck Park flapping their wings, flocking to the *cholito* with the bag of stale bread.

"Eat bird," he said, recalling Keats. "Thou wast not born for death, immortal Bird!"

His stomach churned loudly and he tightened his abdomen to muffle the rumbling.

"Are you hungry?" asked Pepe.

Turning around, he saw Pepe holding out a can of salt peanuts. He hesitated a moment, then his whimpering stomach won out.

"Thank you," he said, taking a handful.

"*De nada*," said Pepe.

He sat back as Juan crammed peanuts into his mouth, hastily swallowing partially chewed bits. Then, at the opportune moment, when Juan's mouth wasn't full, he leaned forward and, trying his best to sound matter-of-fact, asked:

"What did you think of Galindo's 'little speech'?"

"It was ok," said Juan, brushing salt from his cheek.

"Did you know that he omits facts?"

"Like what?"

"Like when he talked about *Los Científicos*, Porfirio Díaz's philosophical advisors. He didn't mention that they were a bunch of racists assholes, did he? It's well documented. *Los Científicos* believed that the Mexican Indian population was inferior."

Pointing to a specific page in *A History of the Mexican People*, Pepe cited his source.

"This one Científico named Francisco Bulnes was quoted as having said, 'Five million white Argentines are worth more than fourteen million Mexicans.' What kind of *pendejada* equation is that? And Galindo thinks that Díaz saved Mexico. *Sinvergüenza*, teaching Mexican history to young, impressionable Chicanos."

Moved by Pepe's indignation, Juan felt a stirring inside of himself, a feeling akin to pride and rage. It rose to the surface of his soul and stayed with him as Professor Galindo clicked a button on the remote control in his hand, dimming the lights and starting the slide show. And everything that Juan now saw filtered through this exciting, new emotion.

The images flashed slowly onto the screen: A black and white photograph of a young Porfirio Díaz, who wore a plain, tweed suit and bow tie, a black, unkempt moustache and the distinct look of ambition. Professor Galindo paused to admire the photograph for what seemed like an inordinate amount of time. Then vast oil fields in Veracruz, owned and operated by British conglomerates; a Mexico City train station, circa 1900, amid a sea of *sombreros*, built and managed by American railroad barons; a huge American mining town in Cananea which, according to Professor Galindo, had grown to such proportions because new technology and mining techniques had made it possible to extract unprecedented amounts of minerals from the land, making millionaires out of foreigners who had come to Mexico penniless.

The new feeling stirred in him again, more intensely this time, could even have been considered xenophobia had he a country to call his own. Seeing beyond the images being projected onto the screen, he looked into the past and witnessed the coming of the Yankee hordes, whole families on horseback, in buggies and covered wagons, moving steadily southward, leaving clouds of dust in their wake, like an invading army, emitting the strange, rasping sound of a new language, a constant, distorted and menacing noise, like that of a plague of locust devouring crops.

And Mammon led them on, he thought, recalling *Paradise Lost. Mammon, the least erected Spirit that fell from Heaven. Even in Heaven his looks and thoughts were always downward bent, admiring more the riches of Heaven's pavement, trodden gold, with impious hands rifled the bowels of their mother Earth for treasures better hid.*

And he thought: *¡Pinche mamones!*

The slide tray rotated, the image vanished, and a new image appeared, an intricate ink-sketch of a bullfight.

"Here we see a Sunday afternoon bullfight at the Plaza de Toros de San Pablo," said Professor Galindo. "The spectacle of this age-old tradition offended English and American tourists and was banned in certain regions of Mexico during Díaz's first term."

Juan had once been to a bullfight in Tijuana and the sight of the ink-sketch brought the memory of it hurling back comet-like, reoccurring in the span of a few seconds.

It was a small arena by the sea. The festive crowd had come to see *El Magnífico Torero de Zapopán, El Gran Matador de Matamoros, El Inconquistable Muletero de Cuernavaca.* Trumpets sounded, the spectators whistled and cheered and the first bull sprung out of the chute, furious and bewildered, into the middle of the ring. The sun had blanched the sand and the brawny, black-glistening bull looked more like a monstrous shadow independent of the object that had cast it, darting wildly across the ring. There was a portly *picador* donned in a purple outfit with gold embroidery, mounted on a gray, dappled stallion, who stabbed the bull repeatedly in the hump with a bright, ribbon-garnished pike, wounding its neck so that it would keep its head low and be more vulnerable when it faced the matador. The bull bled and the sand soaked up the blood, and somewhere in the arena, from *sombra* or *sol*, a drunken aficionado defended the suffering animal, shouted: *"¡Ya! Gordo cabrón! ¡Basta!"* Then, a matador marched bravely into the ring and challenged the exhausted bull. It made many passes, but the spry, young matador dodged the horns and the manic crowd chanted: *"¡Olé! ¡Olé! ¡Olé!"* Slowly, methodically, the young matador pierced

58

the bull with swords, one, two, three to the hilt, until the dying animal spurt blood from its mouth, splashed the ringside wall, and stained the salt white sands. The bull fell, the spirited crowd applauded and the proud, young matador blew kisses and bowed. The people tossed flowers into the ring and mules, indifferent to the task, dragged the dead bull away.

Granted, it was a gruesome exhibition, but Juan was willing to concede that it had cultural merit because it was rooted in tradition. So to prohibit bullfighting to spare the delicate sensibilities of tourists seemed to him extreme, even unjust.

Corridas de toros, he thought, *were too much like ancient, Roman blood sports in the eyes of the tourists. Barbarous games handed down in some form or fashion from the Romans to the Spanish to the Mexicans, inheritance of the conquered. But I suppose every country has its own form of institutionalized barbarism. What if a Mexican tourist visiting the United States in 1947 had attended the baseball game where Mr. Jackie Robison, king of the Negro Major League, crossed the color barrier? And what if the Mexican tourist had watched as that brave and gracious black man trotted onto Ebbets Field and had heard the home fans booing and calling him nigger, had seen them spitting on him as if it were some kind of an ancient, pagan baptism, drenching poor Mr. Robinson in snot and saliva instead of hot bull's blood. Would President Harry S. Truman have banned the Great American Pastime simply because a Mexican tourist was offended by the spectacle?*

Again the slide tray shifted and the bullfight faded from the screen and from memory.

"And the last slide is of Porfirio Díaz as an elder statesman," said Professor Galindo, "white haired and weary, having toiled for more than three decades to improve the lives of the Mexican people."

59

He studied the photograph: Old Díaz in an expensive, sable suit, a well-trimmed, handlebar mustache and a sated face, cold and pale as wax. He heard Pepe saying something about how Díaz powdered his face to mask his dark skin, to look more like a light-skinned European. Professor Galindo, motioning passionately to the screen, was attesting to Díaz's greatness, even as the image of the dictator disappeared.

Yes, Juan mused, *Díaz is a long time in the grave, and yet he still haunts the Mexican psyche, haunts Héctor, the worthiest of men, who has traveled a thousand miles north from Guanajuato and will cross tonight at Sonoita or San Miguel Gate or Sasabe, carrying what food and water he can. Héctor who will walk through the cold night, into the scorching heat of day, avoiding border patrol check points, risking heat exhaustion in the Sonoran desert and death at the hands of vigilante ranchers, because there are no jobs in his home town—since Mr. Díaz invited foreigners who came and overstayed their welcome, foreigners who pillaged and plundered and absconded with millions of dollars and pounds, deutsche marks and francs and left little for the Mexicans. They left very little of México para los Mexicanos.*

Professor Galindo clicked a button on the remote control in his hand and the lights came on again. The students, like conditioned lab rats, stirred from their stupor, gathered their belongings into backpacks, and shuffled down the rows toward the exits.

"That's all for today," said Professor Galindo. "Read chapters ten through sixteen in *A History of the Mexican People.* Don't forget to start reading *The Underdogs* and . . ."

Before he could finish, however, the students began filing out of the room. They weren't listening to him anymore, their thoughts having shifted to the big football game on Saturday afternoon and the keg parties later that night; thoughts of going home for the weekend, of seeing family and of sleeping in. Everything but Mexican history.

Professor Galindo threw his hands in the air and sighed: "Have a good weekend."

Out in the hallway, Juan and Pepe walked leisurely amid a bustling mob of students.

"*Y se supone que Galindo es hombre con educación*," said Pepe.

"*Para tarugo no se estudia*," said Juan.

"You speak Spanish," said Pepe. "Very well."

He sounded like an approving father acknowledging a desirable quality in a son. Juan could not understand why Pepe was so pleased with his ability to speak Spanish. He could only assume that it was due, in part, to his apparent love of all things Mexican. Or perhaps communing in the language of their forefathers afforded them a bit of comfort and solidarity so far from home, creating a kind of cultural buffer between themselves and the other students at the university. Whatever the reason, Pepe's approval appealed to his sense of worth. He liked how it made him feel and so he gladly accepted the praise unthinkingly, as he did the invitation that followed.

"There is a gathering Friday afternoon at Whittard Hall," said Pepe.

"What kind of gathering?" asked Juan.

"The kind *you* shouldn't miss. Have you ever heard of the Mexican-American Resistance Coalition-Heritage of Aztlán?"

He had heard of this Chicano student group as one does hearsay about a stranger. There was some truth and some invention, depending on who was doing the telling. To some they

61

were dangerous young militants, a bunch of barrio supremacists in the guise of college kids. To others they were a legitimate student organization, struggling to maintain cultural identity, while working to bring about positive change by means of education and political advocacy. In reality, he himself didn't know very much about them, other than what he had read in the Daily Kodiak, stories of non-violent demonstrations, hunger strikes for equal rights and sits-ins as symbolic acts of *Reconquista*.

"Yes," said Juan. "Of course I've heard of MARCHA."

"Then you know what we're about?" asked Pepe.

"Yes."

"So I can count on *you* being at Whittard Hall on Friday, right?"

"Yes," said Juan, walking out of Finney Hall into the cold, mid-morning air.

"*Nos vemos,*" said Pepe.

They shook hands, made a pact of sorts, and parted ways.

He remembered the maples all along the college footpath trembling in the wind and dry autumn leaves falling everywhere as he started the slow, steady march back to Chadwick Hall. And although he made a concerted effort not to step on the dead leaves, there were just too many of them and he crushed them underfoot.

6

All the way to Whittard Hall Juan wondered, *what have I gotten myself into?* He was skipping class to attend this so-called gathering and he didn't even know what it was that they were gathering to do up there, in that L-shaped building. Were they laying out designs for a quiet revolution or plotting a bloody overthrow of the government? Whatever the case, he thought it too late to turn back. The hall was within sight and he didn't want to disappoint Pepe.

Around the Ionic pillars of Whittard Hall and pitched rank and file along the high, marbled steps was a crowd of perfect strangers with familiar faces. He had seen them all before at one time or another around campus, eating oranges and reading *The Road to Tamazunchale* at the bus stop on Hayden Street, playing marathon chess matches in Brightmore Commons and waiting patiently in purgatorial financial aid lines in Paley Hall. Now they were all here, on this blustery afternoon, holding protest signs. Juan crossed University Drive, faltered as he approached the hall, searching the faces in the crowd for Pepe, but he didn't see him. Disappointed though he was, he drew nearer still, and when he got up close he studied their slogans.

One sign read: 14TH AMENDMENT *MY ASS!*

Another declared: BROWN POWER v. BOARD OF REGENTS

And yet another, more to the point, demanded: AFFIRMATIVE ACTION NOW!

Only then did it dawn on him what was happening.

Ah, he thought, quite innocently, *this is a demonstration. MARCHA must be protesting the Board's ban on affirmative action.*

His thoughts scattered and digressed.

And where is Pepe in all of this, he wondered, *where has he gone? What's become of young Prince Pepe, the First Son of Aztlán?*

As he pondered this, he was accidentally jostled by a passer-by and he stumbled into the crowd of demonstrators, inadvertently becoming one of them.

"Take this," said one of the demonstrators, handing Juan a protest sign. At first he refused it, pushing it away. It was a heavy thing, the words stenciled on it were heavy, aggressive and loud. It went against his quiet nature, against his inborn desire not to draw attention to himself. But the demonstrator insisted, thrusting it forcibly into his hands, saying again: "Take it!"

He took it against his will and promptly put it over his face like a mask, thinking again: *Where the fuck is Pepe?*

In the sunken quadrangle, out in front of the hall, beneath a crescent of swaying palms, spectators, impartial to the cause of the protesters, had congregated. He peered over his sign at them, like a peeved little boy, begrudging them their right to come and go as they pleased.

Happy people, he thought, *who have everything that they need and so are not burdened with the responsibility of demanding it.*

What if he simply slipped away, into that fortunate crowd, walking backwards inconspicuously, his arrival in reverse? What if he disappeared into them, without looking back? What if he went

64

about his business, returned to the ordinary life he knew before all of this? He wasn't about to start singing freedom songs and burning American flags, only to be tasered and carted off to jail for causing a public disturbance. Nor would he, like a dissident monk, set himself on fire. He didn't want to be a burning martyr. He simply wanted to be loved by burning martyrs.

Looking nervously over his shoulder at the rabble of protesters, he suddenly noticed how quiet they were for a mob presumably gathered to give voice to a cause. Maybe it was a silent protest, he thought, like the one in Tehran after the rigged presidential elections. A powerful and eerie thing to see on the television set: one hundred thousand Iranians marching in solidarity through the winding streets of the capital, without making a sound. Silence juxtaposed to a multitude to shed light on injustice. And the world's eye transfixed on it. Silence so that God Himself would see and come down on their side. No, he decided. This was something else altogether. These students were waiting for someone to come and ignite the day with words.

Up on the landing, set squarely between the entryway pillars, Juan saw an oak podium absent the speaker.

Watch closely, he thought, *somebody's coming to spout beatitudes or something.*

He stared at it, willing somebody to it, hearing Farrington's bells marking the hour, willing something, anything to happen, because the pressure was giving him a headache. And then, before the twelfth gong struck, Pepe appeared out of nowhere at the podium.

My prince! Juan almost sang out, embarrassed by the thought of it.

He watched as Pepe switched on the microphone and set a bottle of water on the podium shelf, fully expecting him to say something emotive and profound to whip the crowd of protestors into a visceral frenzy. But instead Pepe turned abruptly to greet the speaker, who was just now coming out of Whittard Hall, a middle-aged man who moved with the energy of a spry college kid.

¿Quién es este cuate? thought Juan, looking him up and down, trying to formulate an opinion of him. His outward appearance, an amalgam of style, baffled him. He wore a plain white T-shirt and a posh sport jacket, faded denim blue jeans and expensive-looking, suede slip-on loafers. He was bespectacled, clean-shaven and had a queue hairdo, like a Diné warrior. It gave Juan the impression that he was some kind of ex-hippie radical turned intelligentsia-Chuppie, that is to say, a Chicano yuppie academic.

"That's him," said an awe-struck freshman standing next to Juan. "That's Professor Farías. They say he was one of the leaders of the East Los Angeles Blow-Outs in 68' and that he marched in the Chicano Moratorium against the Vietnam War in 1970. They say that he single-handedly got us a Chicano Studies program at this university. He's the man."

Juan began to examine his own thoughts on what he'd heard, not letting it sway him too much one way or another. Meanwhile, up on the landing, Professor Farías talked privately with Pepe, a brief exchange of words, most likely greetings and glad-handing. Then, Professor Farías stepped to the podium with a solemn sort of dignity, and there came a wave of riotous applause from the demonstrators. It went on like this for a while, until at last Professor Farías raised his hands and silenced the protestors. All

66

eyes fixed on this charismatic man as he addressed the people, but Juan's gaze was suddenly drawn to a beautiful girl in the crowd.

She's a perfect beauty, he mused. *Not like some American starlet with a symmetrical face and a statuesque figure.*

Juan had been snubbed by women like that all of his life and had conditioned himself to scrutinize any woman that he found remotely desirable, until every last one of her flaws was exposed and she became ordinary or even homely in his eyes, and the desire left him. But this girl, he concluded, was impossible to pick apart. Everything about her was as it should be. A pixie-like physique, a naturally bronzed body and an obsidian black, bobbed haircut, which in profile accentuated her delicate jaw-line, her dainty, freckled nose and honey colored eyes. Seeing her in the mid-afternoon light of late October, looking like some kind of Chola Dynasty goddess, he got the distinct feeling that she was the kind of girl who would gladly be adored, but would never allow herself to be possessed, and this made her all the more attractive.

As he stared at her he was aroused, but not in the typical, libidinous way. A feeling rose up fiercely, deep within his chest, a hot rogue wind, so strong that it yanked the protest sign right out of his hands and sent it soaring into the sky, like a lost kite. And his eyes, in desperation, went up with it, into the clouds, because with it went his reason for being here in the first place and for now having the privilege of staring at the gorgeous brunette in the crowd.

"Come down," he implored it. "You're making me look bad. Come down now!"

Catching wind and sunlight, the protest sign fluttered and shined as it climbed nearer the stratosphere. Then, seemingly heeding Juan's wispy pleas, the sign wheeled around, dipped and fell out of the sky with Icaristic velocity.

It crashed down on the westside of University Drive, went tumbling end over end and was dragged for two campus blocks by the wind. Juan broke ranks and chased after it, making low comedy out of the high drama of the protest, stooping and clutching at it clumsily, but every time it slipped out of his grasp. Finally, out of sheer frustration, he leapt and planted a foot atop it, leaving a muddy boot print on the E in *Equal Opportunity Now!* Embarrassed though he was, he rejoined the demonstrators on the steps of Whittard Hall and promptly hid his face in shame behind the protest sign.

Professor Farías, up on his mount, digressed and returned to his argument in turn.

"Because I did not come here today," he said, "like a bereaved family member, to mourn the death of Affirmative Action, to eulogize it as one would a dearly departed relative. Though the board of regents has demonized it, calling it a quota system that promotes reverse racial discrimination, and in the end saw fit to kill it, I will not mourn."

Nods and murmured affirmations stirred and rippled through the crowd.

"Nor am I here to state the obvious, to tell you that the underrepresented will be underrepresented, that our numbers here at this university will dwindle, like an endangered species. I will not stand here and use pat expressions like 'inequity of inequities' or Johnsonian inspired catch-phrases like *'You cannot take a man hobbled for years by chains and liberate him, bring him to the starting line of a race, tell him that he is free to compete with the others and rightly believe that you have been fair."*

Juan was listening half-heartedly, straining to capture the words, because in truth his mind was a defective-spider web these days, incapable of snaring any foreign objects. There were far too many holes in it. Of course he'd snatched snippets of Professor Farías' speech, words like *inequity of inequities*, but they slipped through one of the many holes, manifesting as *inequity of inequities that a hot brunette like that exists, that you discovered her, but can't lay claim to her. She's out of your league. Shit!*

He was still thinking about the girl when Professor Farías said something about the historical imperative and how restoration was in order. Coming out of the rosy fog of his fantasy, reacting to apish applause, he quickly hoisted up the protest sign, waved it rapturously in the air and, like a man catching fire, started chanting along with the others:

"Affirmative Action now!"

A compulsory act, really. He was trying to fit in, was actually only mouthing the words, while anxiously searching the slowly dispersing crowd for a glimpse of the girl.

Professor Farías saluted the protestors once more, triumphantly pumping his fist in the air, before turning to go into Whittard Hall. They all howled and cheered, and the freshman standing next to Juan said: "Farías is the *fucking* man."

"Uh-huh," said Juan, distracted, in a panic, thinking, *Shit, where'd she go?*

His disappointment, however, didn't last. It went away, like the scattering crowd, reluctantly nudged along by reason.

"You wouldn't have done anything anyways," he said to

69

himself. "You impotent fuck. You effete motherfucker. You sterile donkey! You don't have the balls to talk to a girl like that. You would've just stood there staring at her, drooling. *God* she was good to look at!"

He stared blankly at the Ionic pillars of Whittard Hall, perfectly majestic in their immobility, and wondered if he shouldn't, like some mad and spiteful Samson, pull them down and let it all come crashing down on him.

Oh, but she might get hurt too, he perseverated, *if she's anywhere near Whittard Hall.*

He thought that he saw her sitting alone on a little stone bench up on the landing, looking so demure, her tanned legs crossed primly, her delicate hands nesting on her lap, like sleeping doves, but it wasn't her.

The look of loss returned to Juan's face and everything that his young heart was feeling poured out and tinged the autumn sky a dusky rose. He was the divinely anointed, once and future king of counterfactual thinking, and now his great and thrilling scheme of winning the mystery girl over with his awkward charm was over. Looking down at his tattered jump boots, he stomped his feet and started to walk back to Chadwick Hall. But a cheerful voice stopped him in his tracks, saying, "Hey, are you looking for me?"

Turning towards the voice, he saw Pepe standing there, grinning, a fat stack of protest signs tucked under his arm.

"Hey, *Pepe*," said Juan, disappointed that it wasn't her.

"Great speech," said Pepe. "That was something. Doctor Farías is Jesus F. Christ."

"Yes," he said, absentmindedly, thinking of the girl. "*She* was something."

"And now we celebrate! There's a party over in Palms."

Pepe handed him a poorly copied party flyer.

"Tonight, nine o'clock. Drinks, music and women."

It occurred to him that the girl might be at the party and that he might get to meet her. Out of nowhere, some Latin saying, as subtle as an arrow in the head, at once archaic and apropos, came to mind.

Dum spiro spero!

He was sure that he'd seen the phrase before, carved on the stone lintel over the main entryway of one of the university buildings or maybe tattooed on the upper arm of some Bohemian panhandler chick down on Venice Beach.

Breathe, he told himself. Hope. And the lighthearted side of Juan put in:

Ok, what has two thumbs and the greatest luck in the world? Me, that's who!

Forgetting all about the politics of the day, and thinking, too, that everything, even the pursuit of love, was political, Juan smiled and said, "Ok. See you tonight."

7

Soon after sunset, Juan took the last No. 12 Big Blue Bus out of campus, traveled eight miles east and presently reached the Palms District and his stop. Using the party flyer as a map, he meandered up and down a series of dark, side streets; lurched along cracked, earthquake buckled sidewalks, beneath flickering streetlights, his lanky shadow nipping at his heels as he approached each lamppost and dashing hastily ahead of him as he left each lamppost behind. He passed row after indistinguishable row of white, two-story apartment buildings with short, yellow lawns and, as the city's name promised, lots of palm trees. There was a moment, after looking for 22 East Palms Avenue for nearly an hour, which he considered giving up and heading back to campus, but the thought of the girl kept him going. He finally found the apartment complex by following the sound of Spanish music, coming from apartment # 219 on the second floor, its windows rattling and its walls throbbing.

This is it, he thought, knocking timidly on the heavy, metal security door, tentative as a nervous door-to-door salesman.

Across the street, an old gray van pulled up nosily alongside the curb, parked under a streetlight and honked three times. From a lightless duplex, the windows and doors boarded up—a structure slated for demolition, a condemned house—a young woman's voice, elated and evidently relieved, called out, *"¡Oye, Chuy! ¡Espérame! ¡Ya vengo!"*

The driver turned up the volume on the radio, lit a cigarette and reclined in the bucket seat; his dark face aglow by the halo of golden streetlight overhead. As promised, the young woman did not take very long. She appeared on the porch and, hurrying across the stony lot, without stumbling once, got into the van. She kissed the driver and they sped away.

How easy it seems to have that, he thought. *How wonderful it'd be to have that.*

It was as close as the invisible crickets twittering beneath the doormat or the tethered dog yelping in its master's yard across the street. It was near, stirring on the sleek black rooftops, but somehow as far away as the most distant star in the autumn night sky.

He knocked again, a little harder this time, while surveying the metal screen door, looking it up and down at great length, studying the well-welded joints, the solid steel rivets, the sturdy doorknob. A well-constructed door, he thought. A good door, though it actually angered him to admit it. Scowling at it, as if it were to blame for his long wait on the doorstep, he proceeded to pound on it.

After a while, the inner door opened. He took a step back, and when the metal screen door swung open, dangling precariously on broken hinges, *the girl* he had come to see was standing at the threshold, staring at him as if he were some strange, wild creature who'd come uninvited in the middle of the night. She was saying something, her lips were moving and her hand gestures were animated, but he couldn't make out her words. Watching the beautiful mime, he felt a sudden shortness of breath and a throbbing in his eardrums. This girl, the image of her at this very moment, in all of her splendor and rage, would be seared into his psyche forever, like a hot iron brand of the letter *x; x* for an unknown and independent thing.

"Kick down the door, why don't you," he finally heard her say, in a subtle, but exceptionally sexy lisp.

"I'm sorry," he said. "I didn't mean to knock so hard."

"I thought you were the cops."

"I knocked once before, but no one opened the door."

"Yeah, well, I heard you. The people across the street heard you. Everybody in Palms heard you."

She was wearing a snug fitting, low-cut, little black dress that accentuated every part of her fine young body and showed far too much cleavage and thigh.

"Come on in then," she said, exasperated.

She motioned him inside and pointed to an apricot-colored futon.

"There," she said. "Sit over there."

He sat down in a daze, shocked and curiously aroused by her cruelty.

God, she's a real bitch! he thought.

He watched her saunter across the living room floor, push her way through the noisy, drunken rabble of partygoers in her stilettos, back to a company of handsome young suitors. Curious, and somewhat threatened, the young men stared at Juan, pointed and asked who he was. The girl shrugged, made a face that seemed to say, "Don't know and don't care." This seemed to set their minds at ease.

Juan, meanwhile, was oblivious to all of this to-do. Quite innocently, he looked around the room, took stock of his surroundings.

This was the house of poor students, sparsely furnished with things picked out of dumpsters and items bought at second-hand stores with money taken up in a collection: a sofa the shade of mustard, the cushions flat as unleavened bread, the stuffing coming out of the arm-rests, gutted by an obstreperous house-cat, a pair of rusty, 1970s baroque inspired lamps, and an end table that looked like a squatting, leprous, hunched-back dwarf. Judging by the hundreds of volumes nestled in the wickerwork bookshelf, he assumed that this, too, was the house of a great mind. Any well-read scholar would be remiss for not stopping to admire such a private collection. No first editions, of course, and none bound in leather, and yet so many good books: Stories of ancient India and Holy Roman emperors, the Russian revolutionary intelligentsia and the Chicano Student Movement, Japanese rock-gardens and Eastern philosophy, the Torah, the Koran, and the Holy Bible, finite mathematics, immigration law, world literature, advanced linguistics, principals of parliamentary procedure, and Deconstruction theory. Everything that a growing young mind needed to sustain profound inquiry and thought. If anything was missing, he thought, it might be found at Perkins Library. His head cocked slightly to the side, he read the titles one by one and drooled.

Dull, warm, golden light emanated through every binding as the books began to float off of the shelves and flutter silently above his head. Dust particles coming off the dust jackets formed a new universe in the musty, living-room air. Amused by the scene, but not surprised by it in the least, he snickered into the palm of his hand and reached out to touch the magical, flying library.

When Pepe found him he was still sitting there, gazing at the ceiling, grasping at thin air, smiling like a baby enchanted by the spinning mobile above its crib.

Juan heard Pepe before he actually saw him, a humming—nebulous words trying to find form, disconnected chatter slipping into his ears, as if emanating from beyond the apartment walls; then an indistinct object, a human form, a head, a torso and limbs, seen peripherally, sitting right next to him on the futon. He was dressed impeccably for the party—gray twill pants, a white linen shirt, black suede oxfords, his fair brown hair slicked with hyacinth-scented oil.

"What are you doing man?" asked Pepe, puzzled and a little amused.

"Uh, nothing," said Juan, coming out of that other place. "I was just adjusting my . . . nothing."

"Well stop it, huh. People will think you're crazy."

"Ok. I'll stop. See. I've stopped."

"Alright, relax. I was just kidding. Can I get you something to drink?"

"No, I'm ok."

"So," asked Pepe, "what're you studying at the university?"

"English literature."

"Why English Lit.?"

"I like to read."

"Shakespeare and shit?"

"Yes, and Chaucer and Milton and Swift and Wordsworth and . . ."

"Have you ever read *The Autobiography of a Brown Buffalo?*"

"No."

"How about *the Revolt of the Cockroach People?*"

"No."

"What about *Pedro Páramo?*"

"No, not yet."

"Well, then you really haven't read shit, have you?"

"I mean, I've heard of those books," said Juan. "It's just that . . ."

"They got you reading all of this other shit. I get it. It's required reading. But seriously, you've got to read Mexican and Chicano literature, too, to learn more about your own culture."

"I will. I promise."

"Ok then."

Juan was distracted, staring across the living room at the girl, again.

"Actually, can I ask you something," he said meekly.

"Go ahead."

"Do you know that girl over there?" he said, nodding furtively.

She was sitting idly on the sofa, encircled by an air of cultivated vanity and an unrelenting swarm of suitors, casually fiddling with her golden bracelets and sipping a cocktail.

"*Her*," said Pepe. "Sure that's Bernadette. Everyone knows Bernadette."

"Bernadette," he whispered to himself triumphantly, believing that knowing a woman's name gave you some kind of power over her.

"Well, does she have a boyfriend?" asked Juan.

"Get in line, brother!" said Pepe. "Her loyalty to any one guy is like her major: Undeclared. Forget about her, man. Have a drink, instead."

"Ok," he said, reasoning, *what better distraction is there than libation.*

"So, I'm glad you came out to the rally today."

"I need something strong," said Juan.

"We had a great turn out."

"Tequila?"

"We made a big difference today brother."

"Or vodka?"

"We set the wheels in motion."

"Vodka," he decided, thinking involuntarily, *the wheels will come full circle and stop.*

Pepe got to his feet and, smiling down at him, said, "I'll get you that drink, now."

He returned a few minutes later, carrying a highball glass brimming with clear liquid.

"*Aquí tienes,*" said Pepe, handing him the glass. "There's more in the kitchen. Help yourself. I got to make a phone call. Be back soon."

"Thanks," said Juan.

He held the tumbler up to the light, examined it from all angles, checking it for insects, hair or saliva. Once satisfied of its purity, he drank.

"Smooth stuff," he said. "No tingle on the tongue, no burn in the throat, no fire in the belly, no alcohol in my alcohol."

Confused, he sniffed the contents of the tumbler.

"This is *water,*" he said.

People were still arriving, coming in out of the cold in twos-and-threes with that aura of anticipation and wild exuberance that people sometimes have before a party. As they made their way inside and were greeted warmly by friends, one of the party-goers made a passing remark about the poor condition of the screen door, saying:

"It's coming off the hinges. Someone should get that fixed."

Juan didn't notice the growing number of guests, so busy was he brooding over the drink that he'd been given, the one that wasn't vodka.

He brings me water, he perseverated. *If I had asked for water, he probably would've given me an empty glass.*

Matter-of-factly, he spilt the water onto the shag carpet, held the empty tumbler in the air, filled it slowly with refracted, whiskey-colored light, toasted himself and drank.

After sitting there for a while, Juan got bored and decided to mingle a bit, resolving not to speak to anybody, wanting mostly just to listen in on their conversations.

He pushed his way through the hot, sweaty throng of dancers in the center of the living room, clutching to his bosom the same drink he'd been nursing all night. It was a tight squeeze, and when he came out on the other end, sticky as a baby lathered in vernix, he stumbled into a corner and was inadvertently pinned in by a human wall—three, great big East L.A. types, Pancho Villa-looking men of prominent stature. They had their mountainous backs turned to him, were not even aware that he was standing there, and it worried him, because they were drunk and could accidentally crush him against the wall, just like that. If it was any consolation, however, the corner, ironically, was an ideal vantage point from which to spy on Bernadette.

He regarded her now, by electric light, saw that she had specks of golden glitter on her lips and dusted liberally along her neckline. The good looking Mexican-American boys were trying to impress her, locked in a contest of intellectual one-upmanship, cataloging the names of all of those professors at the university whom they deemed praiseworthy.

"Farías is a genius. There's no denying that."

"González is good. He knows what he's talking about."

"Yes, and Batista is pretty good. She's very progressive."

"I like Yañez. He has some interesting ideas."

"True, but I get more out of Peralta. In my opinion, he's a real master of the negative method of hypothesis elimination."

"Professor Pérez is a pervert," Bernadette suddenly interjected. "I caught him staring at my tits the other day, right in the middle of his lecture. He looks up from his lectern, ogles *them*, and forgets what he's about to say. It gets worse. I see that he's got this little erection in his corduroys. It's not the first time I catch him looking either. I'm thinking of filing a grievance with the university ombudsman."

She sipped her cocktail and added, "Either that or I'll blackmail the son of a bitch."

The suitors lowered their eyes, and just for a second Juan thought, *how gentlemanly of them*, but then he realized that Bernadette was sitting on the sofa and that they, standing all around her, likely egged on by the power of suggestion, were actually looking down her blouse.

Look away now, he cautioned himself. *Nothing in the world is more dangerous than a beautiful girl leered at, too little or too long.*

To calm his nerves, he guzzled his drink, and by some miracle his cup was overflowing.

Guests continued to arrive, none of whom Juan could see over the heads of the three, hulking young men standing in front of him. Thus, leaning against the wall, with no one watching or even knowing that he was stuck in the corner, he used it to scratch his ass in anonymity.

He let out dull grunts as the itch went away, listening excitedly to the intermingling strains of conversations stirring somewhere in the room and in his ear, like off-camera voices.

"Spaniards are evil, cruel, bloodthirsty, lazy, greedy, treacherous and fanatical . . ."

"People have been telling lies since God gave them tongues and that particular lie, La Leyenda Negra, is a five-hundred-year-old varietal . . ."

"Sure, because a genetic study recently conducted at the Autonomous University of Madrid apparently contradicts claims of absolute Amerindian genocide in the Caribbean . . ."

"Every country, government, commits atrocities . . ."

"Propaganda invented by the English and Dutch during the Protestant Reformation . . ."

"The American version of the Black Legend tells us. . ."

"Mexicans, too, are evil, cruel, dirty, lazy, ignorant, treacherous, conniving, back stabbing and biologically predisposed to a desire to kill or at least draw blood . . ."

He wasn't ready to hear that someone had been spreading lies about him, centuries before he'd even been born. But there was lighter fare in the air.

"Ok, a Guatemalan walks into a bar with a howler monkey on his shoulder . . ."

". . . and the bartender says, 'So that's what makes the monkey howl.'"

From a corner of the room came the savage braying of wild donkeys.

"Here's another one, why do Mexicans cross the border two by two? Give up? Because the sign on the wall says, No Tres-passing!"

"That's a good one!"

"Alright, what do you call someone who speaks two languages?"

"Bilingual."

"That's right, and what do you call someone who speaks one language?"

"Monolingual."

"No, Dumb-Gringo!"

Something about the sound of their laughter disturbed Juan. He got this image in his head of an abstract painting he'd once seen, a quintet of drunken jazz musicians blowing their French horns, their lips twisted into knots, their cheeks inflated like red balloons, their eyes crazed. Yes, that's it, he thought. The source of their laughter was not amusement. It was malice.

He turned his attention toward Bernadette again. There she was, swimming gracefully in a deep and turbid sea of male testosterone, sexual innuendo and disingenuous flattery.

It must suck to be a pretty girl, he thought, to have every other fucking guy trying to fuck you, all of the fucking time.

She seemed to like it, though, like the attention anyhow, like the idea of having a bunch of drooling, gormless brutes at her beck and call, ready hands, erections and all.

Juan wanted to corner her, in a comfortable, well-lit corner, lean in close and tell her how he felt about her, until the sentiment

82

touched her and she felt the same way too. But he wouldn't get the chance. So said the voices. They were talking about him, like conspirators.

"Did you see that crazy looking motherfucker?"

"Who invited him?"

"Don't know. I think he's Pepe's boy."

"How do we know he ain't an undercover cop or something?"

"Remember Professor Farías' stories about FBI infiltration of MARCHA in the 1960s?"

"He's right. This guy could be a rat."

"He looks like a fucking rat."

"He looks like a pinche Arab."

"Yes, he has a face only a mother, an Arab mother, could love."

"He looks like Fadi the Fiend, all skinny and shit."

"Tell Pepe to stop feeding stray dogs."

"Stray dogs are skittish. Chase him out."

"Stray dogs are rabid, too. Careful, he don't bite."

"We could ask him to leave, politely tell him to get the fuck out."

"He looks like he'd go without a fight."

"And if he won't go?"

"Then we kick him out."

"And if he happens to be endowed with the uncanny strength of a lunatic?"

"Then we get the Velásquez brothers to help us."

"Ok, it's settled. We throw his ass out."

Juan was hearing all of this and trying really hard to remain objective. Certainly they had cause to say such things. Did they see him as the singular incongruity, the only visible loose stitch in an otherwise seamless tapestry of normal human faces? Was it the clothes he wore or his seemingly indifferent attitude that made him stand out? Maybe it was the way he held his drink in a death-grip, how he held it closely, guardedly, against his chest, and raised it to his mouth without so much as bending his elbow? Then again, it could have been the way he stared level and blank one moment and then, unexpectedly, how his eyes flickered, beamed and drifted upward toward the ceiling, only to come down again, level and empty. Or perhaps it was the size of his nose. Dear *God* what a proboscis! Why hadn't they noticed it before? An enormous, crazy-looking thing, with nostrils like craggy grottoes and a grotesque curvature of the bridge; a schizophrenic's nose.

By no means did he believe their opinions constituted a professional diagnosis. They weren't psychiatrists, were likely not even psych majors, but they must have considered themselves good judges of character. Good enough to determine that Juan wasn't right in the head and so must be put out of the apartment, because there was no telling what he might do.

He had a sudden and irrepressible urge to piss his trousers. The thought of going in the corner, like a yet-to-be housebroken dog, actually crossed his mind. Then, one of the gargantuan young men standing in front of him shifted his weight ever-so-slightly, an imperceptible movement really, mere inches, but it created a gap just big enough for Juan to escape. Seeing his opportunity, he squeezed his way out of the corner and hobbled down the hall to the bathroom.

Juan locked the door and relieved himself in the toilet. At the sink, he stared at himself in the medicine cabinet mirror. He looked like a man who'd barely escaped being stoned by an angry mob. Running the hot water tap, he let it steam in the basin and fog up the mirror. When it was unbearably hot, he rinsed his hands, soaped and rinsed his hands. He washed them three times, despite the scalding hot water, in accordance with some stringent, hygienic decree. It left first-degree burns, but took his mind off of things. Everything but Bernadette—the incomparable, amazingly ubiquitous Ms. B. She came pirouetting in again, not incarnate, but by proxy. As he stood over the sink thinking about her, a single, shiny black strand of hair descended from above, became suspended in the vapor and dangled indefinitely before his eyes. It turned slow, willowy circles in the faint light, like a music-box ballerina.

The hair had fallen from a follicle on Bernadette's lovely scalp, had manifested in this squalid latrine, as if to let him prove, once and for all, just how much he loved her. This then was Juan's last chance to make a case for love, to recite devotional sonnets like an impotent wooer, to beg for it and, if all else failed, to be met by her midway to love and take her by force.

After a brief, tense moment, he reached shakily for the strand of hair, but quickly retracted his hand and jerked his head toward the door. He thought he heard Bernadette out in the hallway. It was her, alright. He recognized the soft, sexually hypnotic lisp, paying some guy a rare compliment, saying something about the appeal of quiet strength in a thinking man.

God, how good it must have felt to be admired by her! He imagined that Bernadette was talking to *him*, fantasized that she was making overtures at *him*.

"Thank you Bernadette," he said. "That's the nicest thing anyone's ever said to me. You know when people ask me, 'What do you like the most about Bernadette?' I always answer, 'I love everything about her.' But if I were pressed, I mean, if I absolutely had to pick just one thing, if my life depended on it, I'd say that it's her generous spirit that I admire the most. No, that's not it. I think I'd tell them that she's so aloof that not even death itself could touch her. Yes, that's it, that's what I love the most about Bernadette. She's a cold-hearted bitch."

Self-satisfied, Juan grinned and waited eagerly for a retort. And for his vindictiveness he heard her giggle and say, "Come on now, Pepe. Don't be shy."

Fitting, he thought, his mouth twisting into a smirk by the irony of it. But if she chose to throw herself at Pepe, he couldn't really hold it against him.

She can't help but like the guy, he reasoned. *Women like confident, intelligent, good-looking, light-skinned men. Women like sober men, because drunken men are unattractive, and unattractive, drunken men are downright loathsome.*

Juan could not help but feel like a divorcé who was seeing his ex-wife with another man for the very first time, sickened by the fact that he had become her *insignificant* other. He pictured the whole seduction scene, feeling nauseated, but trying hard not to vomit.

She was tugging playfully at Pepe's belt-buckle, coaxing him into a dark bedroom, making it so easy for him, saying, 'Come on. I won't tell if you won't tell. Come on, it's alright.'

He looked up in time to see the strand of hair dangling above the sink suddenly spiral into a curlicue and vanish in a poof of lilac dust.

"Let us think philosophically on this," Juan said, trying to lighten the mood to soften the blow. "You do know what the Buddha said about love, right? He said, 'To hell with you if you can't take a god damn joke!' Actually, I think that was Muhammad."

He lowered his head and meditated for a moment, thinking:

This is the immense paradox that swallows us whole, though we remain wholly untouched. Unrequited love. It is ever present, like silence under the yoke of sound. Love is dried dung.

He sat on the toilet and offered up something less introspective and more to the point.

"God damn all beautiful women, most especially Bernadette. May she go to hell! Amen."

But no one was listening. He was alone. Slowly Juan turned, made a wailing wall of the herringbone patterned shower-curtain and let loose a slew of caterwauls and moans.

8

The memory of those days, of the *Mexican American Resistance Coalition-Heritage of Aztlán,* was lucid in Juan's mind even now, two years hence, and just as painful. He still saw its members on campus now and then, hanging out by Whittard Hall. He had run into Pepe and Bernadette, too, a few months back, down in the Village, crossing Lexington Ave. They were a couple now and were engaged to be married after graduation. As they passed each other on the street, Juan stopped to greet them, but they walked right passed him without saying hello.

That's just the way it is, he reasoned, trying to put things into perspective and out of his mind for good. *Despite cultural affinity, I was a pariah in their eyes. Who knows why?*

Sitting there on the toilet, in the bathroom in Perkins Library, he traced the letters of the acronym MARCHA on the bottom of the stall door with his finger. He was still waiting for the ghostly throng of white persecutors to storm the bathroom. Nobody came and yet he waited, unwilling to step out of the toilet stall until he was absolutely certain that he hadn't been followed. It could very well be a trick. They might be waiting for him, persistent and dreadful as evil spirits, by the ivory white urinals.

"Hello?" said Juan. "Is anyone there?"

In reply, a leaky faucet dripped water into a clogged sink.

"If you're there say something. Don't keep me waiting here

all night. I've got to study for midterms. Hello? Is anybody there?"

He was alone, and to prove it lifted the stall latch and stepped outside. Very much alone, he realized, a grubby, mountain hermit coming out of his cave, scratching his head, thinking that he had heard voices, which were nothing more than woodnotes, the drone of cicadae in the adjacent wood, nothing but the deafening hum of the florescent lights overhead.

He blinked up at the lights, drawing strange comfort from the multiple rows of electric tubes. Steadfast and bright, they murmured assurances, promised him that everything was going to be alright, even went so far as to accompany him out of the bathroom and light his way along the narrow library aisles, through the perilous labyrinth of stacks.

Back at the private carrel where he had been studying, Juan found all of his belongings exactly where he had left them, a perfect snapshot of time gone by: the anthology of English literature, opened to the last page of *The Wanderer*, the little burgundy notebook, a shred of paper coiled in the wire binding, and his cheap fountain pen leaking indigo ink, the blot on the notebook a likeness of a tiny tea cup and saucer. Had he abandoned these possessions altogether, archeologists might unearth them in a thousand years' time and remark what an excellent find it was, and hypothesize that the owner of these artifacts, sensing imminent danger, had fled. But they actually wouldn't have the slightest clue as to what terrible things lurked within the confines of this 20th century university library.

It was funny to imagine such scenarios, anyhow. He collected his belongings and disappeared into the stairwell.

After midterm exams there was a short reprieve. Juan spent most of his time lying in bed, reading old, urine-stained Daily Kodiaks and literary magazines, sleeping for hours on end, stretched out like a cat and skipping the occasional lecture. But by the third day the fear of not knowing whether he had passed or failed caught up with him.

What did it mean to make the grade anyway, to be successful at the university, in a country that worshiped success above all else? Favor and ascendance? Wealth and leisure? A big house in the hills, a luxury sedan and holidays in the sun? Did one's life suddenly become more significant than the lives of those who were unsuccessful? Did the old, Anglo-Saxon maxim, *through deeds that bring praise, a man shall prosper in every country,* still hold water? Or was it, as he suspected, that fortune did not necessarily side with the hardest worker, but rather with the sons and daughters of privilege? The question had gone unanswered in his subconscious mind for many years, because the simple act of conjecture inevitably led to that other question. What did it mean to fail in a country that worshiped success above all else?

Failures went home to their mothers and fathers, hung their heads in shame and did their best to explain what had gone wrong; why everything that they had hoped for had not come to fruition. Failures went home, hung their heads in nooses and did not have to explain a thing. This is how it would be with him. At the end of his last term, he would go home, a registered letter, creased into quarters, tucked into his back pocket, the official blue and gold seal of the University of Los Angeles, California as letterhead, the introduction, body and closing chocked full of ominous phrases like, *We regret to inform you . . . required grade point average . . . all rights*

90

and privileges hereby suspended, and *summarily dismissed from the University.* Homeward, after long, serious talks with college advisors and the head of the English Department himself; home again after an impromptu meeting in a stuffy, cloistered office with a surprised looking dean, suffocating in the air of finality as he was told for the very last time that academic probation was not an option and that nothing else could have been done.

Standing in the smoky warmth of his mother's ample kitchen, the aroma of black coffee brewing in the morning air and a clear view of the rose buds blooming in the garden out back, he'd show his mother the letter and look away. And as she read it, he'd be thinking, *I am the grass that did not grow, I am the barren earth.* But much to his surprise she'd hug him and insist that he move back home, because of her two sons he was the one who had clung the tightest to her skirts as a boy.

Quietly, he'd settle into the old house on Inez Street, and at first it would feel like salvation, but after a while the sense of comfort and familiarity would make a stagnant pond of his once promising young life. He'd never go back to school and never marry. He'd get a job at the Gómez Brothers' Zapatería, and make his living fitting shoes on the tender little feet of the countless children of all of the people with whom he'd gone to high school. Once in a while someone would recognize him in the store, ringing up a pair of loafers or coming out of the stock room with a pile of shoeboxes in his arms and a gold plated shoehorn inscribed, *Employee of the Year,* dangling from a chain around his neck. They'd glance at his nametag to make sure that it was actually him, the smart kid who'd gone off to college, and say to themselves, "What's he doing here? Didn't he get some kind of a scholarship to study at the university?" But the person asking the question wouldn't want to know the answer, because it really didn't matter to them at all. Failures went home and were soon forgotten.

On the appointed day, a Tuesday, according to the official school calendar hanging on his dorm-room wall, he went around to all of the lecture halls, met up with teaching assistants and professors, collected his bluebooks, and quickly retreated to a secluded spot on campus, deep within the university's Japanese garden—a place that only he knew about, a little wooden bench concealed within a thicket of holly. Other than faint footprints in the narrow, dirt path leading there, he left no trace of his whereabouts.

A jay bird, perched in a nearby tree—eyeing the fresh crop of sweet holly berries below—was the only living thing to witness the private moment; a young man with an unnatural countenance, fanning out examination booklets like a winning hand of poker—arranging them and rearranging them to satisfy some queer sense of order—sobbing and mumbling to himself, "C, C, C minus, C. Divine intervention is the old college try. A miracle, a perfect, spring day miracle."

As he sat there sniffling and wiping away his tears, an afterthought came crashing down on him with the force of a tsunami.

Half ass miracle, he conceded. *Professor Sackard's barb in bluebook # 2, written in red ink, written in my blood, erroneous statements, did you do the reading? I read it all, everything on the syllabus, three times; what more does she want?*

By now Juan had spotted the jay bird in the tree and he

addressed it, as he contended with yet another disturbing afterthought.

"What more does she want? Maybe I'm no Rhodes Scholar. God knows, I won't graduate *summa cum laude*. I'll be lucky to get out of here with a *chinga tu madre*. But what gives her the right to cheapen my miracle. Ah, never mind, never mind. It's a miracle anyhow."

He wanted a good, hot meal and a bottle of something strong to celebrate the occasion, but he didn't have the money. And though his first instinct was to sit for hours and brood about it, he remembered the birds. Whenever his father got laid off from the factory, and the pantry was empty, save for pinto beans in a glass jar, and the rent was due, his mother would talk about the birds, how they did not sow, nor reap, nor gather, and still God fed them. He dared not ask it out loud, but as he stared up at the little azure jay in the tree, he thought, *what am I going to eat? What am I going to drink?* The jay cocked its head, seemingly contemplating his predicament.

"Go down to the basement of Dixon Hall," it said, in middling English. "Go to the end of the hallway, the last door on the right, room B-226, Student Loan Services. Go in. You'll have to stand in a line and fill out an emergency loan application. Look over the promissory document closely before signing. It's a standard agreement. If you default they'll call for your big, Mexican head. They'll put a hold on all of your university services. You'll be reported to every credit bureau in the land as a swindler, and litigation will be brought against you in a court of law. But don't worry, don't worry. One hundred dollars, interest free, to be repaid in one month's time. That's plenty of money and plenty of time to pay them back. Not a bad deal, if you ask me. Hand the clerk your student ID and the application. He's going to ask you why you need the loan. Make something up. Tell him that it's for utility bills, textbooks, toilet paper, whatever."

At the sight of passersby approaching, the jay bird suddenly broke off speaking English and cawed. Then, as soon as they were alone again, it said:

"So, what are you going to do with all of that money?"

He didn't have the heart to tell the jay bird that he was going to squander it all; he was going to spend it on fast food and alcohol, just like most people who weren't used to having money would do. But the jay bird already knew this and in all of its grace and mercy simply said, "Never mind, never mind," and disappeared into the lucid, blue sky.

It was quite a simple procedure. The clerk issued him the check, no questions asked, and Juan took it, without considering how he'd settle the debt. He went down to cash it at a prominent bank in the Village, American Financial something or other, a big, white stately building on the corner of Lexington and Dover. Until this afternoon's transaction, he never had reason to go inside. Now, with the draft as a voucher of admittance, Juan marched up the marble steps, passed the row of imposing, Corinthian pillars, through the glass doors etched with a drawing of a flock of golden eagles (which always made him think of people of means, powerful, prestigious people, and left him feeling insignificant), onto the shining floor, to the blond bank teller.

He had made a habit of looking down whenever he spoke to someone with blond hair, especially if it was a female, most especially if she had blue eyes. A learned behavior acquired soon after arriving at the university. Were the days of lynching Mexicans for looking at white women (even the homely ones) really over? He wasn't taking any chances. But now, with the hundred-dollar check in his pocket, he held his head up and boldly looked the teller in the eyes.

"I'd like to cash a check," he said. "A one-hundred-dollar check."

"I need to see two forms of identification," she said.

He reached into his coat pocket and produced a student ID card and a crinkled, black and white photocopy of his birth certificate.

"Will that do?" he asked.

"Yes, yes, it's fine. How do you want it?"

"Small bills please."

He ignored the look in her eyes as she doled out one hundred dollars in denominations of fives and tens, the look that seemed to say that both he and the task at hand were beneath her, a look that told him that she would rather count pennies all day than cash his pittance of a check. *It's not you*, he reassured himself. *She's just having a bad day. Let it go.* He managed to keep up the positive self-talk, even when she slid the bills across the mahogany counter, and snipped, "Take it." He thanked her, took the money, and walked quietly out of the bank.

It was a modest sum of money, even by working class standards. Yet, in the hands of a starving student, it amounted to a small fortune. He wandered happily through the streets of the Village, the money humming in his pocket, singing to him, *"Spend me, spend me, I must be spent, quick as a match stick, every last cent!"* He feasted at Luke's corner hot dog stand and bought a couple of hot

95

dogs, loaded with the works, for a homeless woman who asked him for spare change. He drank one too many beers at a local college tavern, was asked to leave, and picked up a quart of fine American rye whiskey at a convenience store. He priced new shoes at a couple of different shops, but finding none that he could afford marched back to the residential hall in the twilight glow.

Upstairs they were drinking and singing drinking songs. And he, lying down below in bed, shrouded in the blood red sarape, heard every word of it in the walls, a sound as eerie as bad plumbing in the winter.

"Here's to Brother John, Brother John, Brother John. Here's to Brother John who's with us tonight! He's happy, he's jolly, he's horny by golly, here's to Brother John who's with us tonight! So drink motherfucker, drink motherfucker, drink motherfucker, drink!"

This somber serenade was followed by silence, either real or imagined, which gave him time to ponder the fact that he would never *be* beloved Brother John. It did not make any difference how many college degrees he earned, nor how much money he made. He could marry a plain white woman and surround himself with all of the Caucasian friends in the world. His life would never be anything like the life of Brother John. Not that he lamented it. He only pondered it as a matter of fact, as one would the weather report or the time of day. Just the same, he raised the whiskey bottle to the ceiling, made a toast to good health, to the end of midterm exams and to going home in the morning, and drank. It flowed smoothly into his gaping mouth, down his throat, seeped into his ulcerated stomach lining, was imbibed into his already swollen bladder, filtered into his ailing kidneys, and lastly, like a river to the sea, was absorbed into his bloodstream. Afterwards, as always, came the thoughts, flowing just as easily as the whiskey.

Take council with the bottle to forget, he mused. *Take council with yourself, like homesick Odysseus, who wandered, wandered, wandered, lost a decade out at sea and dark the years between, the mind's like that; sailing life away, year after year after year, sailing from thought to thought, island to island, coming ashore, risking death, risking insanity, sail on, sail on, sail on!*

He drank bright drink, terrible drink, sweet and drunken rye, and his mind sailed on. But it returned, in due course, to the knowledge that he was running out of alcohol. The bottle, propped stiffly between his upper thighs, was now three-quarters empty and after every sip he grew increasingly anxious. He wanted to prolong the feeling of not feeling, that self-induced sense of oblivion and bliss. And there, on the table, by phosphorescent lamp light, was enough money to keep him moderately drunk for three days and nights. There, too, knotted up in the fine, green fibers of those bills, was the implicit truth that the money, like all things borrowed, was already spent and owed. The notion of debt was sobering.

Debt like Dicken's father, he thought. *Insolvent debtor sentenced to debtors' prison. Debt like at the end of every seven-year period we will have a relaxation of debts and every God damned creditor will relax his claim on what he loaned his neighbor, but foreigners who've incurred debt may be pressed, so I'm shit out of luck because I don't have a penny's worth of gold dust to my name. Debt like the joke, Do you know the Chicano vowels? E I O U A. Eh, I owe you money a! What do I owe my mother and father, who came to this country, risking death and insanity for a better life? What do I owe that primordial Arab-Spanish-Mexican couple who first conceived me, a thousand years ago? And if I do not pay, will I be a credit to my race or will I be a debt?*

High above, a phone rang and went unanswered. Peals echoed down the vents, into his dorm-room.

"National Credit Bureau calling," said the booming voice on the other end, as if connected to an amplifier. "Where's our money?"

He stopped up his ears with his thumbs and the winds changed direction again. East this time, back to the place where he was born. His bags were packed, his bus fare—three dollars in quarters—was stacked neatly on the lower, left hand corner of the table and his route was carefully plotted out on a municipal bus line map.

The ride home took him from the bustle of a perfect, mid-sized metropolis, with every flower shop, fashionable boutique and cafe, fine jewelry store, financial institution and Protestant church in existence within a three-mile radius, to a simpler, more familiar world. With a sudden jerk, a raucous rumble and a burst of toxic fumes, the bus headed east. He rode in the back, watched the scenery change in quick succession. Green lights, red lights, and traffic, so much traffic. Neat, white rows of luxury, high-rise apartment buildings and Mexican gardeners manicuring the lawns of vast estates. The sprawl of substandard housing and Mexican gardeners tending to their own, modest little rose gardens. He was home at last.

Anna Castillo still lived on San Benito Street. Such a pretty girl, and so intelligent. She was accepted to a small, private college back East, but somehow never left Boyle Heights. Wasn't that something? Anna Castillo still lived on San Benito Street. Nick

98

Gómez was a young, gifted musician, taught by his uncle, who played in a famous *Norteño* band. He owned a cobalt blue accordion with olive green reeds, but hocked it when he was nineteen to support his addiction. Now he was doing time in an upstate penitentiary for armed robbery. He robbed Pete's Pawnshop on the 4th of July. Francisco Molina joined the United States Army right out of high school. A skinny kid, so skinny that when the recruiting sergeant came to Mott Street he brought a bunch of bananas to bulk up poor Pancho, so that he'd make weight. Bananas, yes we have no bananas! They sent him to the Middle East to fight for freedom and he never returned. They say his mother went crazy with sadness. Héctor Sánchez, the drinking champion of Jullien Street, lost the big bout with alcohol. Stories of cirrhosis of the liver, coughing up blood, and how he moaned for water as he lay dying. Only twenty-nine. Too young. Much too young. They buried him in a family plot in the Evergreen Cemetery. There is a little niche carved into his grave marker with a snapshot of Héctor before he took up drinking. Age eleven, dressed for Holy Mass, smiling lovingly at someone standing behind the photographer. And what ever happened to Norma López? Did she squander her beauty on mirrors and thankless men? Yes, she married Arturo something-or-other after all. They became the lost young couple that lived on Dundas Street, *Donde Street*. They had relations and begat three, dark, beautiful babies. Then Arturo, stud horse that he was, took a *sancha* and begat two more dark, beautiful babies.

Happy are the sterile, he thought, staring sadly at the bottle between his legs, *who've abandoned all hope of fruition*.

He finished the last of the whiskey and rolled over onto his side. Whatever strength he had was now gone. All-night study sessions, poor diet, heavy, episodic drinking and the dark, ever present cloud of pessimism had taken it out of him. Tired, too, of the solitary life he led, of talking only to himself, and of calling upon ancestors who never answered. When he pictured his family tree, he saw a black cypress, the overlapping tendrils etched with thousands of names in microscript, tapering down to catalogued twigs, branches and boughs, where scion was grafted to stock, down to the ancestral trunk, further still to petrified roots and black, immemorial soil. Far more ancestors, he realized, than living relatives. Didn't they owe him a little something, for surviving this long on his own, out here in the wilderness of American academia, for staunchly defending the family name against all comers, real or imagined? Perhaps, and yet not a single one of them would come down now to comfort and guide him. How did the saying go?

When you go, you will be remembered, but only until those who remember you go.

It wasn't that way at all. It was he who'd been forgotten by dead loved ones. Or maybe the host of spirits that he prayed to had simply dissipated into a dark, unknown plane. Either way, they did not answer him. He grunted and rolled onto his side.

Upstairs they were chanting hundred-year old limericks, stories of sexual exploits and the consumption of vast quantities of ale, voices so loud that the little green banker's lamp on his table flickered and dimmed. It was at that moment, between the failing light and absolute darkness that *he* appeared unto himself. It wasn't a glimpse of his own reflection in the dusty mirror, but a full blown vision of himself, standing outside of himself in the middle of the room, bold and defiant as Cuauhtémoc, the last of the Aztec kings. Dark and handsome, he wore a satin, baby blue

100

boxer's robe, emblazoned with red roses and prophecies. He sat up in bed and smiled, welcoming this pleasant, if unexpected visit.

"Don't despair," he said. "You don't have to worry about a thing. As long as I'm here nothing in this world can harm you. Under my protection you can go anywhere, do anything and be anything."

"But I'm nobody," he said. "I'm not even a—*I'm nothing.*"

"You are everything. *Everything.* Look," he said, pointing to the bottom of the boxer's robe.

At first he couldn't believe what he was seeing: image after vivid image of days to come, flashing, fading, constantly changing against the soft, lustrous backdrop of pale blue satin. It seems that he was destined to become the quintessential career man. Spurred by ambition and an unrequited love of money, he'd establish himself as the senior editor in a big, New York City publishing house. Now a lawyer, now an advertising executive, now a professor of rhetoric. No, that wasn't it at all. He was seeing something else, something much simpler, something having to do with—*yes,* he would go home and teach high school English. Students would respect him because he could elucidate even the most difficult passages of Chaucer, Milton, and Shakespeare. And they'd love him because when asked to sign their yearbooks he'd write kind, encouraging words, telling them that they had that indefinable *it,* and that they deserved all the success in the world.

So, he thought, it wouldn't be such a terrible existence after all. He rolled onto his side and the feeling that his life wasn't his own left him. Anything was possible now, even happiness.

9

The very first thing that greeted Juan when the bus doors parted was the Boyle Heights' sun, which was unlike any other sun. It wasn't the quality of light which made it so unique, but rather the way it illuminated this little, eastside neighborhood; the way it touched the roof-tops of tenement buildings and turn-of-the-century homes, and how it glimmered in the fresh, green crowns of palms and streaked across the pot-holed streets. It was in the way that it warmed his tired brow as he stepped onto the sidewalk (a duffle bag filled with dirty laundry slung over his shoulder), and how it kept him company, like an old school chum, as he floated up Inez Street.

The house that he used to live in—a plain, two-story, canary yellow Victorian with large bay windows and a shady, wraparound porch—sat on a half-acre plot of land at the far end of the block. The architect, the builder, and perhaps the families who had lived in the house before his family—whether they were White, Molokan, Japanese or Jewish—knew exactly how old it was. To him, the house had always been there, rising up from the slanted piece of earth, up through the tall grass and the weeds, between the wild figs and citrus trees, like a Pre-Columbian ruin. Juan hadn't been back since winter intersession, but felt no great urgency to go rushing up the steps and knock on the front door. He wasn't particularly fond of homecomings because, as he saw it, they only lasted until you left again, and if those waiting for you at home weren't equally happy to see you it left you feeling bitter. And so he stood transfixed on the dewy lawn, let the early morning sunlight dawdle on his face, stared at the house and remembered. Memories, diluted by time, hit him in waves, warm and lucid at first, then cold and cloudy.

What was it that his mother said to him on the day he left for college? *Qué Dios te bendiga. Qué te bendiga Santo Tomás de Aquino.* She blurted it, actually, as if with a final breath, and made the sign of the cross on his forehead, pressing down hard with her thumb. God's blessing upon him, but who was the other fellow that she had mentioned? Ah yes, St. Thomas Aquinas, the patron saint of students, to whom you prayed: *Pour forth your brilliance upon my dense intellect . . . grant me a penetrating mind to understand, a retentive memory, method and ease in learning . . .*

If she only knew. And his father, standing curbside? What was it that he had said? *Qué no se te olvide . . .* but a jumbo jet airplane flew overhead just then, and the presumably good advice was lost forever.

At the window, a small hand parted the drab curtains to reveal, and quickly veil again, a woman's soft, rosy, pear-shaped face.

"¿Mamá?" he blurted, coming out of the dream.

She had been waiting for him, pacing the house since sunrise, room by room, and calling it her daily work. In the kitchen she washed the breakfast dishes, swept, mopped and waxed the linoleum floor, and organized the pantry. In the bathroom she scrubbed the baseboards, the toilet, the tub and the sink with industrial strength cleaning products. She vacuumed the entire house, upstairs and downstairs, the stairs too. She washed every window with lye soap and boiling water and dusted the dark drapery and the velvety, paisley patterned wallpaper. With a key that she kept in a coin purse, she unlocked Juan's bedroom door, aired out the must of many months, and lit votive candles. Lastly, she put on a fresh pot of coffee and a kettle of beans. Everything was in order by the time she saw him standing out on the lawn. Through the open window she called to him, her voice barely a murmur, and yet the curtains billowed.

"*¡Cht-cht! ¡Oye! ¡Ven aquí!*"

Always the obedient son, Juan went inside.

His mother, who always wanted a son, who bore him hemorrhaging into the world without so much as a whimper or a plaintive moan, drew him near and squeezed his hands until the blood drained from them. She was a small woman, not much bigger than a girl, and in her milk-white smock and black, French braid completed the picture of youth.

"*Deja verte,*" she insisted, looking him over to see if she had gotten him back in the same condition that he was in before he left for college. It was too soon to tell. What was obvious, however, with his sunken cheeks and his ribcage showing through his threadbare T-shirt, was that he was malnourished. She used to ring a bell at the end of the night and announce to the household: "*La cocina está cerrada.*" But today the kitchen was open and she led him there gently, to fatten him up with a hot, home cooked meal.

Using no press, his mother made tortillas by hand. She patted them flat, rounded the edges into perfect circles and, slipping a sheet of wax paper between each one, stacked them neatly on a wooden butcher's block dusted with flour. It was the very same ritual that Mexican mothers had been performing for seven thousand years or more, making hot tortillas in caves somewhere in southern Mexico, for sons returning home from the hunt; the sweet smell of maize escaping through a narrow crevice in the rock, luring them out of the jungle with their obsidian tipped spears and their kill. Hot corn tortillas for the sons of East Los Angeles, too, coming home from the War in Southeast Asia with broken spirits, cracked minds and Purple Hearts in lieu of limbs. Handmade tortillas for the college boy sitting at the kitchen table, who'd come home twelve units short of a bachelor's degree and a few ticks shy of losing his mind. Therapeutic tortillas to fill his belly, nourish his soul and get him talking, because he hadn't spoken a word and his mother had so many questions. Was he eating regularly and did he wear the pea-coat that his father had bought for him at the army surplus store? Had he made any friends and had he been taking his medication? How were his studies going and what did he plan to do after graduation?

After he eats, she decided. It was no good trying to talk to him now, because at the moment he was playing with a hen pepper shaker, moving it strategically across the table as if it were a chess piece. It was part of a set which his mother and father had received as a wedding gift. Porcelain rooster and hen salt and pepper shakers. The rooster, however, had gone missing some time ago, and although he didn't like to dwell on it, he still resented it. What right did the rooster have to disappear when its place was here beside the hen? Could that which was unsavory be eaten without salt? Capon! Capon! Capon!

Juan looked out the window, surveyed the back yard. It was cluttered with castaway furniture, salvaged from dumpsites, and alleyways—all of it overlaid with mud brown tarps and the promise of restoration. He listened for the sound of sawing, chiseling and hammering.

"*¿Y papá?*" he asked.

She stopped making tortillas and the beans, simmering to a boil, rattled the kettle top.

"*Salió,*" she sighed, not quite an accusation nor a lament. It was quite possible that she knew exactly where her husband had gone to, but didn't discuss his whereabouts, because it would remind her that he, like the youngest son sitting at the kitchen table, had been away for far too long.

She pan fried the pintos in lard and served him up a big steaming mound on a large, earthenware platter, with the freshly made corn tortillas.

"*Buen provecho, hijo,*" she said.

"*Hijo de la chingada,*" he said.

"*¿Qué?*"

"*Nada nada. Gracias, Mamá.*"

He was thinking of his father, thinking, *salió, sal, frijoles sin sal.* He peppered the beans and ate, jamming fistfuls wrapped in tortilla halves into his mouth, swallowing without hardly chewing, eating without hardly breathing.

After breakfast Juan went lumbering up the stairs, his footsteps heavy like a man on a death march, looking gallows grim, even as the fair and gentle light of day, flooding in through a stairwell window, touched him. It was the mountain of beans sitting in his stomach and the effect of the previous night's drinking bout that slowed him down. It was the weight of being at the university and having to ponder the endless number of questions posed

106

to him, about English literature and careerism, about the limbo that was Chicanismo, the state of the human soul and God. Far from that other world now, he didn't want to *know* anything. He simply wanted to *be*. He wanted to lie down on his old bed, sleep for days and forget about it all. The mattress was comfortable, the bedding soft and clean. Light wind rattled the window shade, exposing sunlight on the sill, and just outside, in a nest beneath the eaves, baby house sparrows were chirping. He slept and dreamt of singing birds.

Night came creeping around the far corner of the earth, accompanied by all of the sounds most conducive to the darkness—chirping crickets, dogs barking incessantly, drunken man-voices crooning Spanish love songs, and a whistling *cholo*, a rare sort of bird common to these parts. Awakening to this magical time in a semi-conscious daze, he drew the window shade and stared out at the moon.

Full cold moon, he thought. *The brightest, biggest full moon of the year, as close as it gets to us in its elliptical orbit.*

There was a rabbit sitting in the middle of it, an uncanny likeness created by shadows on the surface and contrasting light. To the ancient Mayans it was a vision of the moon goddess caressing her beloved pet rabbit. To Juan, tonight, it was a resplendent satellite bearing an ominous mark—the hare, born naked, blind and helpless, was now a hairy, omniscient, fully grown monstrosity, prophesizing madness, echoing Professor Kennington's prophecy. There was no getting around it. The things to come were fixed for him, like the constellations in the nighttime sky. And yet there was something comforting in having some idea of what would happen next. He winked at the moon and the All-Seeing Rabbit winked back.

Doing exactly as fate intended, he went downstairs. The house was dark and still, a mausoleum were it not for the two hearts beating in tandem beneath this one roof. The other heart, his mother's, was burning, pulsing, and whirling nearby, in absolute darkness. He couldn't see her, couldn't see the affectionate glint in her soulful brown eyes, but she, connected to him by a divine, maternal artery, knew exactly where he was at all times; she knew his heart, too. On a cool, spring evening like this one she'd want to sit with him at the kitchen table, over hot, lemon tea and gingersnaps, and talk about the things that mattered in life, as old married couples often do; but she knew that he had other plans, a young man's plans, which could not be changed for the world. As he lurched blindly down the hallway and into the bathroom, she resisted the temptation of calling out to him from wherever she happened to be, from the ubiquity of motherhood.

He locked the bathroom door behind him, turned on the light and met his own reflection in the medicine cabinet mirror.

You made it, he thought, smiling gloriously, as if he'd made arrangements with himself to meet by the bathroom sink on this particular April evening, at a quarter past ten p.m. *I'm here, now what? We're going out tonight, comb your hair. My hair? What about your hair? It looks like a pigeon's nest. Yes, I see what you mean. We should cut it. Shave it all. Start over again.*

The decision made, he rooted around beneath the sink, indiscriminately knocking over cans of cleanser, half empty bottles of bleach, hair products, old curling irons, a shoe shine box and rolls of toilet paper, finally pulling out, like a mole yanked writhing from its hole, a little brown serge sack. Undoing the knot, he emptied out the contents: electric sheers, blade attachments and an oil tin, equipment given to him after high school by his Uncle Gabriel, the self-taught barber who hoped that Juan would follow in his footsteps. His famous selling point was this: "It's a good, honest vocation, profitable, too, because people's hair only stops growing after they die. In theory, you'll have customers for life." It made him laugh to think about that now. Upon the faux-marble sink-top, he set the attachments in an ordered row, oiled the steel teeth of the blades, untangled the cord and plugged in the electric sheers.

It *is* too long, he reassured himself, measuring the length once more by eye while undressing. He was always talking himself out of haircuts. A strange, unduly regard for what amounted to an outgrowth of the skin, though he would argue that he wasn't attached to his hair, so much as it was attached to him. *It only stops growing after you die.* The buzz of the sheers was deafening and the vibrations numbed his hand. He grimaced and put it to his head.

Two hundred shekels lying there on the floor, he calculated. And he hadn't even touched the crown. The hair fell like ash and dusted the linoleum.

"*Pelón, pelón, cabeza de melón,*" he said. "When I'm done I'll look like my father did the night he crossed the river."

He was remembering, in perfect detail, the time that he had overheard his father tell the story, the previously untold story, of the first time he journeyed north from Colima and made the perilous crossing into the land of dreams. In the cracked, gold-speckled mirror he could see, like a still frame of the past, his tormented father, driven out of bed by bad dreams, gasping for air, dripping sweat, his brown skin glistening. In the never ending, ever-diminishing sequence of refractions within the infinity mirror, he could see his long suffering father, leaning naked against the kitchen sink, guzzling lukewarm tap-water to quell an unquenchable thirst. Like a distorted echo in a well of time, he heard his father's belated voice, hushed and desperate, telling the kind of story that fathers do not tell their sons, because to recall such a story would cause intolerable suffering and humiliation. He had survived the harrowing ordeal once, but to relive it might very well kill him. And so, Juan told his father's story for him, verbatim.

One thousand one hundred kilometers on foot, from el pueblo donde nací to Matamoros. I did not, as some pendejo once suggested, paddle to America in a barrel, across the Gulf of Mexico. No sir, I walked all the way in my huaraches. I didn't tell a soul I was leaving either, except for mi mamá. In our little kitchen, in the blind darkness of pre-dawn, she kissed me goodbye, made the sign of the cross over me, and whispered marching orders into my ear.

You will be a wandering Mexicano, she said. Go to America, live there as an alien and become a nation, great, strong and numerous.

She didn't cry, because there was no time for sentimentality. To have done so would have been a betrayal. It might have confused me and make me rethink my duty. So, with these few words and a canvas sack packed with fresh corn tortillas, a little cold meat, a little water, spare clothes and a family photo, she sent me on my way. It was the last time I saw my mother alive. She left the world soon after I left Colima. Come to think of it, she may have already been dead when I left, because her voice sounded so faint, like she was calling to me from a faraway place, beyond the autumn quilt of corn fields, beyond the hills, the mountains and the sky. No, she was alive.

Ah, my memory is bad. So, I went walking up the dirt road, until I came to the big, god-of-an-oak tree that stood at the edge of the village, the same oak that had once been an accomplice to a suicide. Silvano, the cabinet maker's son, hanged himself from a middle bough on that tree, that day in late October 1952 when the sky looked like the world was coming to an end. A bloody, sinewy, apocalyptic twilight sky, as if it were being torn asunder from the earth itself. Yes, because the world was ending for poor Silvano. God only knows why he did it—maybe depression, a love affair gone badly or maybe he lost faith in God, I don't know.

Looking up I saw, amid the snarl of serpentine branches, the bough, which mysteriously had turned as black as tar. And atop it sat a familiar shadow, snickering and mocking me in a wispy voice.

¡Oye joven! Death is waiting for you in El Norte. You may as well hang yourself from this oak right now and save yourself the trip.

¡Vete al diablo! I shouted, and left him sitting up there all by himself. I felt bad about that afterward, but he shouldn't have taunted me. I went walking into the village, knowing that he would not follow me, that he could not, because he was stuck up there in that big oak, for the rest of eternity or until God Himself or the Devil said: Ok, get down now. It's time to go.

It was dark at that hour and so quiet. You see, this was before electricity, so there were no street lights to guide me. But there was a full, hallowed moon lighting my way. Everyone was sleeping, even Pedro's dog who barks through the night. The whole world was sleeping, except of course for the chirping crickets, who wake the crowing rooster, who wakes the world. I crept silently along the sidewalk one last time, peering in through the darkened shop windows.

First, La Carnicería, with its chopping blocks waxy with fat and sprinkled with bits of bone. I thought I saw, by candle-light, Braulio the Jowly Butcher, dark chin-whiskers, blood-smudged apron and heavy, razor-sharp

111

cleaver in his bloody hand, hacking away at beef tongues, cow brains and the innards of slaughtered beasts, butchering a large side of pork, sweating and grunting like the dead hog lying on the slab once had. Hoisted high above the shop's rooftop was yesterday's red flag, a sign to all of the customers that there was fresh meat for sale.

Next door was La Panadería, cold as the tomb at this hour, but warm as a mother's love when the ovens are lit. The display cases lay empty, not a crumb, waiting patiently for Don Federico the Baker to fill them up with trays of pan dulce and hot golden loaves of daily bread. Don Federico, who had giant hands, powerful hands from kneading dough all of his life, was stirring on his cot in the back room, dreaming of baking the perfect loaf of bread, mixing flour, milk and honey, rolling out soft dough, molding it into shape and breathing life into it with fire and amor. The cold, sooty ovens were beckoning to be lit, longing to burn and shed a little light in this great time of darkness. It was time to make the bread and light up the world.

Around the corner was La Cantina, a sad, dark hole with empty chairs, empty bottles and empty lives, where hard working men went after work, and before work, and sometimes during work to forget about work. Toil is Man's Curse, that's what they say, but my father always called labor a blessing. Yes, it is a blessing, and so I'd go to America to toil for America.

When the men had finished drinking, or rather when the drink had finished them, they sometimes staggered next-door to La Peluquería, where Próspero, the Evangelistic Barber, sat them down one at a time in his barber's chair and preached to them about temperance, whispering salvation into their ears, Take heed to yourselves, lest your hearts be weighed down with drunkenness. The only thing that those men ever went away with was a bad haircut, because they couldn't keep their drunken heads from swaying. Keep still! Don't move your head!

112

Between the rows of ancient shops and modest little houses, between the endless night and the coming of day sat El Mercado, where people went to buy things and barter for things and sell things. This is where I was first sold on the notion of going north. One morning I bumped into Bernardo, my father's old compadre, and as always he looked happy to see me, but also surprised and somewhat disappointed.

What are you still doing here? he said. You should be in Los Estados Unidos, living like a king. I got a brother who lives in Chicago. He says que hace un chingo de frío up there, but if you can bear the cold there's plenty of work and riches to be made.

How do I get to America? I asked innocently, scratching my head.

You walk north, he said. Look for the river. América está al otro lado del rio.

A tremendous wind blew just then, swept the dust from the empty market bins and battered the stripped canopies. It was the very same wind that had stirred up the thoughts of going north in my head on the morning I ran into Bernardo. I would go north and God willing return some day, a rich man with stories of my travels in Gringolandia. And one sunny morning, in the winter of my life, while picking out a ripe papaya in El Mercado, I, too, would sell some young Mexicano on the promise of the American Dream.

Nudged by the wind, I walked on, to La Iglesia de San Cristóbal, to pray for a safe journey. You see, they built that church to honor Saint Christopher, the patron saint of travelers and immigrants. The story goes that he helped some people across a raging river, and that among them was the baby Jesus Himself, long before He could walk on water. Can you believe it? What if Saint Christopher hadn't been there to help those people cross the river? Jesus might have drowned! So I stopped on the church steps, stared at the great, whitewashed bell-tower with the iron botonée cross on top and I prayed:

113

San Cristóbal, I know about the people who've gone before me, los migrantes desaparecidos, those who were swallowed alive by El Río Bravo del Norte, those who perished in the heat of the Sonoran Desert, those who el hambre y la sed se los tragó, and those who met their death at the hands of evil men. They suffered, died and were buried in immigrant graveyards, all along the United States-Mexico border. Thousands upon thousands of mounds, but no one ever visits them, because their graves are unmarked. Watch over me, San Cristóbal, that I may survive. Watch over all of those who will go after me. Grant us all safe passage to Los Estados Unidos. I pray, en el nombre del Padre, y el Hijo, y el Espíritu Santo, Amén!

He must've heard me, because at that moment the angels and saints appeared unto me, not august and somber-looking like in those paintings on the grotto walls, but meek and cheerful, a family of happy peasants, smiling and waving goodbye.

¡Adiós! they sang, their voices chiming church bells. ¡Qué te vaya bien!

You see, leaving home is often a necessity, my son, and it is never an easy thing to do, but when you have a legion of seraphim and holy saints at your back, when you have family at your back, farewell is just that, kind words, well wishes and sentiments, loved ones telling you, Be not afraid. Go forth. You shall fare well. So I set my sights on America and boldly walked away from the village I had lived in all of my life. I followed a path of my own making, to Tecalitlán, Los Reyes, Jacona, La Pierda de Cabadas, Salamanca, Jaral de Berrio, Zaragoza, Cuidad del Maíz, Palmillas, Tampiquito, Burgos, Anáhuac, and finally to Matamoros. One hundred and eleven days afoot, in my old huaraches, though at times it felt as if I'd been lifted up by divine, benevolent hands and placed gently by the riverside.

On the sandy banks of El Río Bravo men, young and old, from as close as Matamoros and as far away as Honduras, stood watching the twinkling lights of Brownsville in the near distance. They were waiting to cross the river

114

and stared in dread at the savage, black waters, pondering the depths of it, the unforgiving current, perhaps thinking exactly what I was thinking, *Why would anyone even try to cross the river if they didn't have to?* After standing there for what seemed like an eternity, a dark skinned boy named Juanito, who had traveled all the way from Chiapas, came forward and quietly suggested that we link arms and wade across, using the luminous glow of fireflies on the other side as a beacon. It was as good an idea as any, and so we linked arms like brothers, and in so doing bound our lives and fates together.

Against all odds and in opposition to the instinct for self-preservation, we plodded into the river. Baby steps at first, baby Jesus steps, up to our ankles, up to our knees, then suddenly up to our necks, trying desperately to keep our heads above the cold, black water. Downriver we drifted, one thousand meters a minute, like driftwood caught up in The Flood, spinning circles, and going under, clinging desperately to uprooted thicket and going under. Down there, among the fish, the waters were calm and eerily silent. The only sound that we heard was the gurgling of air bubbles leaving our lungs. Down there one of us, the chaparro from Chiapas, lost his grip and nearly drowned, but at the last second I snatched him up by the shirt collar and yanked him to the surface. You see, the river was indifferent to our plight, to our very existence. It did not care what living things we were, man or beast. It only knew that it was El Río Bravo del Norte and that we, like any other foreign object that happened to fall into its waters, intentionally or accidentally, would go down and vanish from the face of the earth, forever. Ah, but we would not go down! No, we would not go down!

By now the light of the fireflies across the river had faded, but I did not despair, because at that moment a beautiful Mexican starling with colorful feathers—verde, blanco, y rojo—a species long considered to be a pest in the Republic of Texas, appeared unto us. Invisible though she was in the new moon sky, we heard her flapping her wings and chattering above our heads.

115

Her song grew louder as we drifted east to the Gulf of Mexico and continued from a fixed position on the other side of the river. Now I don't put much stock in augury, but on that night I swear to you that God Almighty Himself sent us a little plumed angel to sing for us, Here I am! Swim to me! Swim to me with all of your might! Swim to me to save your God given lives! It was a sign and we heeded it, swam with all of our hearts, guided by the song of the Mexican starling. And somehow, somehow we made it to el otro lado, all of us alive! Crawling onto the sandy banks of the mighty Rio Grande, shivering wet and gasping for breath, we looked up and saw our feathered savior, the Mexican starling, perched atop a laurel tree.

¡Ah, joyous noche! We'd reached the other side, exhausted, but alive! We stared back in awe at the onrushing river. It was chocked full of debris, bits and pieces of row boats, old tires, leaves, branches and entire trees, a dead coyote, and sticks, so many little black sticks, a river of sticks, like the one in Greek mythology. It could just as easily have been us floating lifeless out to sea, like little black sticks. It was a miracle that we had survived, a perfect autumn miracle!

Out in the Texan wilderness the stars were so bright that the midnight sky looked like a new dawn. Little sparrows were larking in the mesquites, the air was warm and sweet as papaya, and the ground that we lay on was softer than our own beds back home. And wet as we were, we did not have to build a fire, because each of us was cozy inside with a feeling of well-being. This was the land of dreams. The land of lechita y miel. What was their slogan? Land of the free, home of the slave. I never understood what that meant. Maybe it's like two sides of the same coin, or like two realities in the same country. Yes, because dreams and nightmares are opposite sides of the same coin. This, too, was the land of nightmares. There was something ominous in the air, an indistinct, unpleasant odor wafting in the breeze. Something was coming, far away, but drawing closer.

116

In the distance we could hear rustling and the harsh, guttural sounds of a foreign tongue. Jack rabbits perked up their ears and scurried into their burrows, poisonous snakes slithered into the thicket, and scorpions sought refuge beneath the rocks. We hid belly down in the dirt, in a thick briar patch, put our ears to the earth, and listened: Horses. Six horses. Six gringos on horses. La Migra or maybe Los Rinches de Tejas, neither the lesser of two evils.

They rode up swiftly, white men on black steeds, wielding rifles and devil-may-care attitudes. I saw, by their dark green uniforms, their Stetson hats, and golden badges, that they were border patrolmen, the indefatigable defenders of the imaginary line. They trotted along the riverside, looking for the tracks of illegals, because our kind was unwanted, because our kind (not to draw distinction between our kind and human kind) was not welcomed in their country. One of them, a young, grim-looking patrolman who couldn't have been much older than me, saw something in the mud. He dismounted, knelt down, and examined a series of foot prints, our foot prints. Feeling the crust around each track to determine how long ago we had passed, he finally looked up at his fellow patrolmen, his wild, blue eyes blazing in the darkness, mumbled a few, unintelligible words of English, and mounted his horse. They galloped towards us, trotted along the edge of the briar patch, so close that we could smell their breath, an awful stench, like a dog three days dead, like el aliento de La Muerte!

How do you drive a bunch of Mexicans out of a briar patch? This was their conundrum, even though some of us were not Mexican at all, but Central American. Because of the thorns they wouldn't come in after us, but because of their arrogance they would not wait until we starved to death. Tell me then, how do you drive a bunch of Mexicans out of a briar patch? Do you give up? They fired their .30 caliber carbines into the air, to put the fear of God and the United States government into us, to draw us out into the clearing, and damn it if it didn't work! Gun-fire burst above our heads, echoed in the valley and up the river, terrifying the boy from Chiapas. Cold and afraid, he trembled, made the briar patch shake. He stirred in the dust, whimpered like a trapped animal, and pissed his pants.

Vámonos, he moaned.

Tranquilo, Juanito, I said.

No, no, nos van a matar, he insisted.

Nada va pasar, I promised.

A lie, but it did not matter, because he had already made up his mind. He rose up from the briar patch, thorns gashing his brow, cutting his pant-legs to ribbons, and ran bleeding and screaming into the night. What else could I do but run after him, to save him and to save myself. The others ran, too, scattered in all directions, and the six horsemen came galloping after, hooting, cursing, and mocking us in middling Spanish:

¡Córranle, cabrones! ¡Ahí viene La Migra!

They were not sorry for what they did either. They didn't seem to be worried about going to hell or anything.

And so, my son, the coin of human dreams and nightmares had been tossed into the air, had landed on the sandy banks of El Río Grande, nightmare side-up, and landed us all in a detention camp, a riverine station just south of Brownsville. It was a kind of borderland limbo, a bleak, ten-acre plot with a fifteen-foot-high barbed-wire fence and big brown tents. All of the captives were denuded, deloused, and dehumanized. And for some reason, I don't know why, they shaved our heads. They sat us down in the dirt, like a bunch of submissive lambs, bound our hands behind our backs, bound our feet, too, and blindfolded us and . . . and . . . ah, my memory is bad!

Juan ran his hand across his head and the hairs bristled like quills.

118

"Pelón, pelón, cabeza de melón," he murmured, grudgingly. Low and mournful, it sounded just like a dirge. This Mexican children's song had turned on itself, would never again be the innocent rhyme chanted by the neighborhood kids teasing the boy on the block with the freshly shaved head, on the first day of summer. It had become the wicked verse of the interrogator, played on a continuous loop at a low and needling frequency, in the ear of the captive, the unresponsive immigrant who spoke no English, the one who'd been captured half a mile north of *El Río Grande* on a cold, dark autumn night.

What he had seen in that cracked, gold-speckled mirror was enough to drive any good son to tears, madness or revenge. Of course Juan knew that it was not a sin to cry, or to lose one's mind, but he wanted so badly to rid his heart of all the dark, vengeful thoughts and obliterate the words, "Your countrymen will pay," from the human lexicon.

He sat for a while on the toilet, bitter and exhausted from having walked all the way from Colima with his father, but hopeful that a hot shower and a bit of fresh, Boyle Heights air would give him second life, because he planned on going out tonight. With an air of determination, he got to his feet, brushed the spidery black clumps of hair from his shoulders, swept the floor, and packed away the barber's kit. Then, almost as an afterthought, he drew the shower-curtain, stepped solemnly into the porcelain tub and imagined the hot water coming down on him to wash it all away, the memory of hardship and the remnants of a bad hair-cut alike.

After a long hot shower, the bathroom was covered in a mist so thick that he had to question whether or not he was dreaming. Was he walking in the clouds, high above the world, at last detached from all of mankind? If it was a dream, he wasn't alone. His mother was in the dream, rapping lightly on the bathroom door, asking if he was going out.

"*Sí, Mamá,*" he said.

"*Bueno,*" she said. "*Aquí te dejo la ropa limpia en la perilla.*"

The doorknob jiggled and nimble foot-steps receded and quickly ascended the stairs. Only then did he crack open the door and snatch the clothes which she had left for him. But it wasn't his clothes. It belonged to his father: khaki pants, a button-down, flannel shirt, and undergarments, all of it six sizes too big— the clothes of a giant man, not a skinny college kid. Heavy as swaddling clothes, he knew that it would be cumbersome to wear, realized that putting it on would be like dressing a broom-handle, like draping a skeleton in a collapsed circus tent. But what choice did he have? He put it on.

Out in the hallway, his old jump boots were waiting for him, steadfast as a couple of old army buddies, saying to him, "Let's go man! You're young, and life is so damn short."

"Okay," he said. "Let's get out of here."

He put his boots on, made his way to the front door, and looked back once more, into the blind depths of the darkened house.

"*¿Mamá?*" he said.

She had been watching him all along, gazing at him affectionately from a dark corner, from the ubiquity of motherhood, picturing somebody else altogether, waiting for him to say something chivalrous and sentimental like, "You shouldn't be left alone tonight."

"*Ya me voy,*" was all he said, as he walked out of the house.

120

"*Adiós,*" she said. And the blood pumping in the shared, maternal artery, connecting mother to son, murmured, *Yo te seguiré cuidando desde donde me encuentre.*

10

The Widow Doña Delfina lived right next door to the Bitols and in the neighborhood she was said to be a *bruja*, and all that this implied. Not a sorceress, not the kind who cast spells. Her powers lay elsewhere. Day or night you could see her standing by the large, bay window at the front of her house, dressed elegantly in her best, black satin gown, a scarlet shawl and a crown of miniature red roses in her silky white hair—half hidden in shadow and the dusty, scarlet drapes, peering at the people passing by. She wasn't *metiche* or a gossip, but somehow had a mysterious way of simply looking at people and knowing everything about them.

When the Widow saw Señora Sandoval's teenaged daughter walking to the bus stop last week, she knew that the girl was on her way to the community clinic, where a young, Jewish doctor would tell her that she was indeed pregnant. What's more, she knew things that the doctor couldn't possibly know, like that in nine months' time, on a chilly December morning, she'd give birth to a fat, big-headed baby boy with fetal alcohol syndrome named Carlos.

Doña Delfina also knew all about Don Tiburcio Ochoa. He was the dapper, white-haired old gentleman who strolled around the block at dawn with a brass, lion headed handle cane in hand; she knew that though he looked fine—wore a brand new, dun fedora, a fashionable, three-pieced suit and shiny, wing-tipped shoes—his heart was broken and he was in mourning, because he had recently lost his beloved wife of sixty-three years to ovarian cancer.

And so, when Doña Delfina saw Juan walking by her window tonight, all dressed up like a common gang member minus the tattoos, she knew that he was actually a college student who'd come home for spring break; knew that he was going to meet up with his older brother Richard at someone named Lucio's house. But as he passed by, she sensed something unnatural in that monstrous cranium of his that disturbed even her own, unflappable sensibilities. She couldn't put her finger on it right away, could only see that it was something deep-seeded and that with every tick of the clock it grew bigger and bigger, swelling up in his head like an aneurysm, like a chronic sickness—*ah*, the kid was going crazy and was nearly there!

Caught completely unaware, she gasped and vanished into the gasp, disappeared into shadows and the plush, scarlet drapery, into a past immemorial and a future yet unseen by everyone but the Widow Doña Delfina herself.

Juan moved along the moonlit sidewalk, skipping over cracks and side stepping fire-hydrants, in wholehearted pursuit of the full, April moon which, to him, was now a big white, helium balloon. It floated along in the breeze, bouncing lightly on the warm, springtime current, and he went hobbling after it, holding his father's pants up with one hand while clutching at the invisible string with the other. In defiance of the doomsayers, he would pluck the moon right out of the sky, snatch up the ancient, All-Seeing Rabbit by the ears, snap its neck, and defy all of its dire predictions. His life would change forever, because he'd see that it actually meant something and that he could live it in a relative state of sanity. Hell, he might even go on to live a charmed existence, like the white kids at the college. He took a flying leap, missed the moon by a quarter of a million miles and landed awkwardly on Lucio's front lawn, with his father's khakis down around his hairy ankles.

I wonder if Lucio has a little stepladder that I can borrow, was his only thought as he pulled up his father's pants. The moon rose high above the rooftops and slipped behind a colossal blue spruce; he had to crane his neck to keep sight of it. He might have stood there all night, too, and well into the dawn, if the tall, shadowy figure hadn't come out onto the porch and called him by name.

"Is that you Juan?" the dark figure howled.

"Yes, it's me."

"Are you sure?" it asked, leaning drunkenly against the railing. "You've been away for such a long time at that *pinche* school. You might not be yourself anymore."

He recognized the voice and the friendly banter.

"Yes, it's me *Lucio.*"

"What're you doing out here?"

"*Nada.* I was just . . . I thought I saw a starling."

"A what?"

"Never mind. Is my brother here?"

"Yeah, he's inside. What's with the clothes?"

"It's my father's," he explained, gazing at the moon as it went up and out of his reach.

"You got a ladder I can borrow?" he asked.

"A what?"

"Nothing. How about a drink?"

"Come on in, *puto*."

Up there, on the smoothly polished, whitewashed porch, with the moon rays gleaming off of the planks, Lucio came into the light, face first, biologically young, but old and wise in street years. He had brown eyes that told of how circumstance and poor choices had kept him from being a law abiding citizen, that told of his prison time, too, and how it had made him a hard man, but not inhuman. He still fed stray cats, spoke kindly to small children and dying addicts alike, and would, without fail, serve as an interpreter for any Spanish-speaking immigrant who asked him for help. So, when his best friend's little brother, the collegian, showed up unexpectedly and came lumbering up the stairs, he grinned affably through his piratical, black beard. But the smile quickly sank when he got a better look at Juan.

"What happened to you out there, at the college?" he wanted to know.

At first Juan didn't say anything, because his mind was still on the moon. Then the question registered in that part of the brain that answers and he suddenly felt like the young soldier coming home after the War, being asked if he'd killed anyone. What was he supposed to say?

It wasn't anything like the state penitentiary Lucio, but neither was it a country club, at least not for me. Do you want to hear what it's been like living as a second-class citizen at a first-rate, American university? Do you want to know how I lost piece after piece of myself, which is to say that I am not myself anymore?

"College isn't for everyone," Juan finally said.

There was a time when he would have felt compelled to

clarify such a vague statement, but now, with his mental capacity rapidly failing, he left it up to supposition. Drawn to the sound of gentle, familiar voices and the warm, comforting glow on the other side of the screen door, he went inside without saying another word about it.

Their backs were turned to him. Even so, Juan knew that the one hunched over on the stool, naked from the waist up, with scoliosis and a back like a mural, was Pablo, because the art work was one of a kind, as vibrant, complex and exquisite as the finest barrio mural or museum piece—an intricate, flesh and ink tapestry depicting all of human history, the Loom of Time, the Cosmos, magnificent, hummingbird and plumed serpent gods, enigmatic Aztec glyphs, La Virgen de Guadalupe and her darling son Diego, infamous Mexican revolutionaries, martyred union organizers and the consecrated names of dead homeboys. Then there was the other one, skillfully putting the needle to Pablo's left shoulder, his older brother Richard. People called him *El Gato,* because he had striking, green eyes and was always combing his lustrous, black mane of hair.

"Look who's back from the dead," Lucio announced to the room.

Richard half-turned, smirked and said:

"What're you doing here? Ditching school or what?"

"No, I'm just back for a few days," he said. "Time off for good behavior."

"Vacation, huh? Must be nice. Does *mamá* know you're home?"

126

"*Mamá* knows everything."

Pablo, meanwhile, wanted desperately to see who had walked in.

"Who is it?" he asked, trying to catch a glimpse over his shoulder. "Who's here?"

"Don't move, *cabrón*," said Richard. "It's just my little brother. He's the smart one in the family, isn't that right? He's been up at the college, learning everything there is to know about white people. He's going to become a white man and come back and save all us poor Mexicans someday. Isn't that right school boy?"

Richard meant no harm. It was just his good-natured way of welcoming home his little brother. It was the jovial spirit in him, making light of an all too grave world. And Juan, supposing that perhaps salvation very well might lay in humor, smiled, did as the tattoo of dualistic drama masks on Pablo's lower back suggested: Smile now, cry later.

Drink, drink and be merry, he thought, staring at the shimmering bottles of liquor lined up on the coffee table. Lucio served him a *Cuba Libre* in a king-sized goblet, which he readily took because, as he saw it, the alcohol would make everything seem more laughable and help him forget about the All-Seeing Rabbit and Kennington's prophecy.

Trying not to spill his drink, he sat down quietly to admire Richard's handy work; fine art pieces by a self-taught master of the art of tattooing. Every illustration told a story. This one had yet to be told. It sat secretly in Pablo's soul until he mentioned it to Richard, specifying exactly what he wanted and why. And when Richard agreed to do it, the blue-prints appeared magically in his head, like stars in the sky, in the dying light of dusk.

The little machine purred in the palm of Richard's hand as he moved it in short, measured motions, as he drew a dark, indelible outline, stopping now and then to dab excess ink and blood with a handkerchief. Little by little the new tattoo took on recognizable form. At first it looked to Juan like an inverted, black heart, shriveled up and bled dry; then an abandoned, brittle shell of a beehive, all honeyless and hollow; then it was a rotting pear, forgotten in the dark corner of a pantry. All of these things seen through eyes unaccustomed to the light of optimism, struggling to perceive anything cheery and life affirming. What Juan was actually seeing was something completely different, at least in design, yet exactly the same in essence: Youthful fingers, slightly bent, fingernails, polished and pared, rutted knuckles and finely drawn buttons and shirt cuffs. Hands. A young man's hands, pressed palm to palm. Praying hands. It meant that someone had died, that someone important in Pablo's life had been murdered. To show homage, Pablo was having this image, permanent as death itself, painted beneath his skin. It was the same old story. So-and-so was walking down the street one night, minding his own business and some crazy fool shot him, pop-pop-pop, and so-and-so bled to death on the sidewalk.

It always comes back to this, he concluded. *In our lives, there is more sorrow than joy.*

Some chose to have their grief tattooed onto their bodies with every pigment on the palette, for all to see. He wondered if there wasn't something cathartic or transcendent in sharing your heartache in this way with the whole world. Perhaps it's why tattoos were illegal in prison, done in secret, when the guards weren't looking. At least this was the story he'd heard Lucio tell. Jailhouse tats undermined institutional control of the body, mind and soul. *Tatuajes*, he claimed, had the power to liberate a man from the most dismal cell, in the bleakest penitentiary on the planet. If so, maybe Juan would get a tattoo tonight, across his skinny, brown back, Loco, in Old English letters. Maybe then he could return to the university, the institution of the fortunate ones, where he first took ill, his mind at last set free of paranoia and delusions of persecutions. A village purged of plague. Forget that the Church considered tattoos a defilement of the body, a mortal sin punishable by everlasting damnation. Forget the biblical passage that warned against tattooing oneself. The map to heaven was drawn on the skin, in black onyx ink # 11. Encouraged, he sat up straight, like a man waiting in a barber shop whose turn had finally come, and was in the act of saying, "I'm next," when Pablo interrupted.

"So, what's it like up there, at ULAC?"

"It's hard," said Juan, reluctant to talk about it, thinking, *it's another country, Pablo.*

"You got to hit the books, huh?"

"Yes," he said, *and I don't even know the customs or speak the language.*

"But I bet the scenery is real nice. Plenty of green hills and buildings like churches. Students sitting under shady palm trees, thinking about math problems, history and, what-do-you-call-it, *evolution*, the mysteries of the universe, that kind of thing. Oh, man, and all kinds of pretty white girls riding their bicycles around school, huh?"

"Yes," he said, letting Pablo daydream awhile, thinking, *but the people aren't very friendly. Sometimes they look at me confused and afraid, like I'm a lion that escaped from the city zoo. Other times you'd think that I was a ghost, because they don't see me at all.*

"It sounds good to me," said Pablo. "You know, last night I saw what's-her-name on TV, the President's wife. She was being interviewed by a reporter in Baltimore, who kept calling her *The First Lady of Literacy.* He asked her why she thought education was so important, and I really liked what she said. She told him that it's a ladder to opportunity and happiness, and that everyone in this country, rich or poor, has the right to an education, and I started thinking that maybe I'd go to college someday."

"You in college?" said Lucio. "You can't even read, in English or in Spanish. You're a bilingual illiterate."

"I can read, a little."

"Oh yeah? What does it say on the front page of that newspaper?"

"It says Lucio is a big *pendejo.* Anyway, like I was saying, I want to go to school. Richard even promised that he'd help me learn how to read. Isn't that right?"

"Sure," said Richard. "I'll teach you how to read. Don't move. I'm almost done."

"Then I'll get my GED and go to community college. What do you think?"

Juan didn't answer right away, was momentarily distracted by the sight of a pair of twisted, gray rabbit ears encircled by a lunar-nimbus. They appeared ominously at the kitchen window as a sign that the short, peaceful reprieve had ended and that he'd once again have to contend with the moon and all of its grim prophesies. Not just him either, but the others, too, though they

130

didn't even know it yet. The great white moon was murmuring fortunes in the wind, an inaudible hum that wheedled its way into his brain and forced him to be the bearer of bad news. It spun around on its axis and postulated:

You will be a prisoner for the rest of your life, Lucio, though the parole board has deemed you a rehabilitated man and has granted you freedom; though you are gainfully employed and pay taxes, you will always be a prisoner of other people's perceptions and your name will always be synonymous with the word 'criminal.' And you Richard, who survived the U.S. Army and have always dreamt of owning your very own tattoo shop, rest assured that this will never come to pass. No banker in his right mind will lend you a pinche cent, because you already owe more than your life is worth. No one wants to see you prosper. As for you Pablo, stop dreaming. College is for the rich and the literate. You are destined to work as a high school janitor until old age, until the day that you die.

"No Pablo," he finally said. "College isn't for *you*."

He wanted to explain, to tell them that it wasn't him doing the talking and that he would not willingly discourage anyone from the pursuit of happiness, but the moment slipped away. Eternal tenths-of-seconds during which Richard looked at him as if to say, *you are not my brother. You are the scorpion that lies in wait inside of a man's shoe.* It was even too much for Lucio to hear. In spite of his own sarcastic sense of humor, he knew the boundary between light-hearted taunting and cold-blooded pessimism. He left the house, went out to the porch to smoke a cigarette. And Pablo, who was well-accustomed to being told what he could and couldn't do, hung his head low and said nothing at all.

Nothing to explain and absolutely nothing to forgive, thought Juan, *because the All-Seeing Rabbit has reared it hairy, snaggletooth maw above*

131

the moonlit windowsill, grinning knowingly at me, peering into the well of my soul with its one, omniscient and altogether indifferent eye.

That eye, the unrelenting eye, was a mirror in which Juan glimpsed his own reflection, saw what was going to happen next, saw himself getting unsteadily to his feet and walking to the kitchen, where all things past and all of the things yet to come crossed paths, met at the not-so-happy median.

You'd think that I had lost something of great value, something irreplaceable, thought Juan, shuffling blindly around the kitchen in the dark, painfully aware of his manic behavior, but helpless to control it. He was gazing wildly in every direction, looking for something that was not there. It was not in the dust, deep down in the linoleum cracks, and was not hiding behind the delicate curvature of the plainly carved kitchen chair legs. It had not stuck to one of the many magnets on the refrigerator door and definitely had not slithered into one of the empty beer bottles atop the oval, kitchenette table. *It* was gone and he didn't even know it. Gone before he had a chance to think about the implications, like a decapitated head staring at its lifeless body in the millionths of a second before losing consciousness, incapable of thinking, *I've lost my head.*

He let it go for the time being, but decided to stick around just the same, in case *it* appeared tonight, rather than risk a chance encounter when he least expected it. Luckily then, or unluckily for him, he was the type who could out wait death itself, because Life, that mean-spirited, iniquitous little bureaucrat, had conditioned him to accept, without apology or explanation, the unnatural, yet unalterable order of things; some people had to wait longer than others. So, he came to rest by the sink and waited.

Here he had a first-rate view of everything under the moon—Richard in the next room, concentrating with religious zeal on finishing Pablo's praying hands, and Lucio's lush, backyard garden, a lunar landscape overrun by a colony of feral cats—everywhere cats, Persians, Siamese, Tabbies and Calicoes, in the branches of the drooping willows, among the budding, springtime roses and mating lackadaisically on the back porch, in the broad moonlight. And the ever-vigilant moon, suspended in its orbit, obsessively watched Juan.

Pulling up his father's pants to keep them from falling down around his ankles, he was suddenly transfixed by the shrill, irregular and oddly electrical-sounding twitter of a cricket, which was actually the death rattle of a malfunctioning smoke detector. Still uncertain of what he was hearing, he laughed and suddenly fell silent. He looked elsewhere, followed with deep, personal interest the random path of a cockroach, which had crawled half-way across the kitchen floor and stopped, for a second, ten minutes, an hour, a life time. A sad parody, this: two of God's lowest creatures sat in this kitchen, staring silently at each other in the darkness, both of them waiting for something yet unseen. He shut his eyes and thought, *enough of this, I'm going to count to three and when I open them everything will be revealed, one two three,* but it did not appear. What he'd come to see wasn't there.

Grunting his disapproval, he soldiered on, took a swig from his canteen, sucking cold, coppery water straight from the faucet, while the broken disposal unit belched the foul odor of rotten papaya, spoiled milk and bad fish.

"*Papá*," he gasped, spinning around. "You're home at last."

His father sat defiantly at the table, hunched over and bitter as an indentured soul, indignant at having been summoned back to this unhappy place again, and by his son of all people. His pigheaded father was in the air, pervasive as any volatile, atmospheric element or a lost spirit wafting in between two worlds. He was in the backyard, buried under a mountain of castaway furniture, salvaged from abysmal dumpsites and endless alleyways, all of it overlaid with thick, brown tarps and the age-old promise of restoration. Back again, a fact corroborated by the constant sound of sawing, chiseling, and hammering.

"You come back, *now*," said Juan, neither accusatory nor empathetic, "having receded into the mysterious shroud of the old country, where time does not exist and sins are forgiven by the gods of our forefathers. You return not-so-triumphantly from outer space, having traveled light-centuries from the cosmic center of M-61 or some other cold, whirling galaxy, where you were the only living thing and where, in the silent vacuum of eternity, you had God's undivided attention and you talked to Him and sorted things out. Wherever it was that you went to, I knew you'd come back some day. So tell me, since it's just the two of us, why'd you leave?"

If his father wasn't so busy counting nails, nuts and rivets, dropping them one by one into empty oyster tins, he might have answered.

"Is it because this great country of theirs, which you nearly died getting to, drove you crazy? And so anywhere but here became your sanatorium? Is that what happened? I'm not after a confession *papá*. I just want something to hang onto, an idea, a few details, something to wrap my brain around so that the next time you go missing I won't wonder why. What exactly was it then that made you go crazy?"

There was no reply, but it wasn't because he was being ignored. It was just that his father was presently engaged in a heated discussion with his tools and his sawhorses.

From what he could gather, the handsaw's teeth weren't sharp enough and the sawhorses were suffering from rot wood and were ready to be put out to pasture.

"Was it the long road to this so-called paradise, across primordial, mosquito-plagued marshes, rocky, snow-capped mountain ranges and plains that went on and on and on? Was it the river, when you crossed it for the second time, under an inauspicious winter moon and a multitude of curious stars that had gathered to witness the spectacle? You came out of the water on your hands and knees, crawling to the USA. Face caked with mud and freezing, you rolled into a deep arroyo and curled up like a fetus to keep warm. You might have died of hypothermia, too, if you hadn't found that half-empty bottle of cheap port. Who knows how it got there. Someone, in one of those provincial border towns, must've tossed it in the river and it ended up in the wash, or maybe the last border crosser who slept in the ditch left it there for you, so that you might suffer a little less. Small miracles in the American wasteland. It kept you warm and alive. But the cold still haunts you to this day. It's why your hallway closet is filled with dozens of brand new coats. Fine, special occasion camel hair and everyday synthetic alike. A row of never worn coats, just hanging there. Coats and coats and more coats. Enough coats for a thousand immigrants and all of their children. Was that it, *Papá?* Was it the cold?"

"*¡Dame un clavo!*" cried his father. "*¡Un clavo!*" He heard heavy hammering and wailing, "*¡Ay, aguántate!*"

"Then again it might've been culture shock that led to your failing mental health. When you first got here you didn't speak a word of English or know any of the customs. The only thing you knew were myths about America and Americans, stories told by starry-eyed men who'd traveled north and had returned to Colima with greenbacks lining their pockets and dollar-signs dancing around their heads. The United States of America, they said, is the wealthiest nation in the history of the world. Everyone is rich, even the poor. They've made it so that avarice is not a sin at all, but a virtue, so that even the sparrows, when you toss them a chunk of stale bread, stuff their little beaks, until they're mostly fat and not feathers. Plump little American sparrows. Envy, too, a saving grace in this land, because it breeds ambition in the lazy underachiever, in all of those who would sleep through this golden-age of prosperity and waste their God given right to get rich. Americans work very hard and like to brag about it. Ask anyone of them or don't ask, just listen in on their conversations. You'll hear them say, in so many words, *We are women and men of iron wills and constitutions, who go waltzing through an eighty hour work week without so much as a sigh or a disparaging word* because you see, they've got that Yankee Can-Do Spirit, that inbred, inerrant knowledge in them that says, with the impregnable faith of an expectant mother, while frothing patriotically at the mouth like a Spartan father, *You are an American, go forth and do great things, make lots of money, be happy, everything is possible.* Americans invented him, the New World god

136

of everything possible. Can you believe the gall of these people, the irreverent genius of these people? They've actually conjured up a god who will answer their every prayer, on demand! Can you imagine that? They get what they want when they want it, because it's what they've come to expect. And this god of theirs lives inside each and every one of them. So, all across this great land, beneath these spacious blue skies, rising up from misty, fruited plains and ambers waves of grain, there are a quarter of a billion living, breathing American temples, housing and worshiping the lord of infinite possibilities, of instant gratification, that almighty, Yankee Can-Do Spirit."

"*¡Dame otro clavo!*" his father howled. And again the hammering and agonizing moans, "*¡Ay, ay, aguántate, aguántate!*"

"The thing is," said Juan, "some Americans are very protective of the relationship that they have with their god and all that he bestows. They turn into an agitated swarm of wasps when anyone, any outsider that is, tries to get some of what they've got. You and I have both seen it happen. They'll shout obscenities, stir public sentiment against it, pass laws forbidding it and have even been known to resort to physical violence. To be fair though, it's still the land of opportunity, so you might very well get your chance, but first you have to leap through about a million different hoops. Red-hot, flaming hoops and rusty, barbed-wire hoops, sphincter-tight hoops smeared with animal feces and invisible hoops that you didn't even know existed. You have to prove that you are of good moral conduct, like every American citizen. You must know why the Pilgrims came to America, who the first President of the United States was, and how many stars are on Old Glory. You must speak the King's English without an accent and sing the

Star-Spangled Banner in perfect pitch. You must walk, talk, act and think like an American, adopt an American state-of-mind, work hard and become accustomed to the maddening routine required to sustain the good life. And, as if this weren't enough, you'll have to pledge your dying allegiance to the United States of America and then, maybe, you'll be granted an audience with the Yankee Can-Do Spirit, the American god of miracles. It's enough to drive any man crazy, don't you think?"

"*¡Un clavo más!*" his father pleaded. The steel mallet came down hard and his father wept, "*¡Ay, aguántate! ¡Ay, aguántate! ¡Ay, aguántate!*"

He glimpsed the moon askance and noted that it was now the flat, black-iron face of a universal clock ticking time away, moving Juan closer to the not-so-distant future and a certain, unavoidable fate. A kind of resignation, quiet as cancer, settled in.

"What worries me *papá* is that they say it's"—he whispered—"*hereditary*. I think I've got the sickness, too. I, the youngest son, being of unsound mind, am bequeathed all of your earthly possessions, all that you've suffered, the ugly amalgam of injustices, pain and suffering, fear, loneliness, uncertainty, sadness and failure, everything that broke your optimistic heart and made you lose faith in mankind and God; everything that made you go crazy. God, why couldn't I get good looks, money and confidence instead? Why not a survival instinct stronger than that of a wounded lion on the African Serengeti? Why not sterling sanity?"

Juan waited patiently for an answer, expecting no reply, thinking, *how do you say rhetorical question in Spanish?*

"What can we do," he grumbled. "Prehistoric men drilled holes in the skulls of the sick to cast out the evil spirits. Modern men self-medicate, swallow mouthfuls of psychotropic pills and go about their daily, humdrum lives. Others take their own lives and obliterate thought for good. No! Impossible! The mind, the immaterial mind, like the soul of man, is immortal. Our collective memory will not fade *papá,* and the sickness will go on without end. Nothing to be done now, but wait for it. Wait for it and when it finally comes grin and bear it."

Around midnight Richard walked into the darkened kitchen and found his little brother standing naked by the sink. His father's clothes were folded neatly at Juan's feet and his head was haloed by the full, April moon.

Like the ebb and flow of an ocean tide, Juan was blabbering, in crescendo and decrescendo, *"¡Ay, aguántate! ¡Ay, ay, aguántate!"*

11

The timeless question, posed by crotchety old drunkards rousing at midday, shell-shocked soldiers on the battlefield and the dead when they get to where they're going, was on Juan's tongue as he stirred and sat up in bed. "Where the *hell* am I," he asked, coming woozily out of an apparent fugue. There was no other way to explain it. He couldn't call it a dream, because dreams didn't end this way. And besides, he was still wearing his father's clothes.

"I'm home again," he said, thinking, *but not quite home.* That fact having been substantiated, the next question, logically, was, "How did I get here?" Someone or something must have brought him here. Loyal, kind-hearted Richard who believed, above all else, that turning your back on family was the worst sin imaginable. Or maybe it was the scheming, All-Seeing Rabbit that wanted only to see Juan live long enough to inherit his father's fate. Perhaps it was his father's defeated ghost, who wasn't strong enough to survive the American dream, but still had a little bit left in him to put his ailing son on his weary back and carry him home. The answer was immaterial. He was here now.

It was morning and just outside, in a little, pine-needle nest tucked under the eaves, new born house sparrows were chirping. Hazy, mid-morning light was coming into the world and in through his open window like the delicate and mysterious glow found in cathedrals at daybreak, light emanating not from the sun, but from another source.

"Brand new day," he said, clearing his throat. "And it will end in one of two ways."

It would be life or death for him today, as it would be for anyone else awakening to a world so unpredictable. The only difference was that for Juan it would be a conscious choice.

Life or death?

Don't do it, his will whimpered. It was dying and he would let it, because it meant nothing to him now. There was nothing connecting him to this world, to the United States of America or to the Republic of Mexico, to his god-forsaken family or the Anglo kids at the university, absolutely nothing between his short, uneventful life and that of the freshly hatched sparrows chirping in the nest beneath the eaves. It was clear that he had no future to speak of, only memories drawing him into the past; imaginary pebbles in a shoe, which the obstinate mind held onto with dogged tenacity, as if they were actually worth something, as if they were precious diamonds.

He considered it awhile longer and finally decided that on this day he'd shake the imaginary pebbles out for good. With that, he went downstairs to have his last supper.

In the quiet fold of his mother's big, sunlit kitchen, with absolute abandon in his heart and a terrible rumbling in the pit of his stomach, Juan laid open the fridge doors and, forsaking utensils and table etiquette, started devouring everything inside of it. He snatched up handfuls of Spanish olives and shot them into his mouth one after another, rapid as machine-gun fire. He swallowed whole the three beefsteak tomatoes sitting on the top shelf and felt them roll smoothly down his throat—one-two-three—like freshly smothered parrots going down an anaconda's gullet. He ate beans straight out of the pot, quarts of pintos sopped in syrupy brown juice, and then had a go at the pork and homily stew. Naturally there was a thick, gelatinous layer of fat coating it. He ate that, too, letting it melt on his tongue like chocolate. And even though he hadn't saved any room for dessert, the tray of sweet watermelon wedges went down easily enough. Resting the tip of the tray on his lower lip, he tilted it slightly, opened his mouth and down it went, seeds, rinds and all.

It was the kind of meal that sleepwalkers eat in their sleep—a dreamer's feast, a banquet for an unhappy beast. What will the coroner say, he mused, when he dissects my distended belly and discovers that mishmash of half-digested foodstuff? He'll scratch his big, pink, bald head and note, with scientific detachment and uncharacteristic, boyish curiosity, that in all the years of doing autopsies he'd never seen anything quite like it.

He'd eaten so much that his father's khakis split at the seams and the fly wouldn't zip. And the plaid shirt, once six sizes too big for his slender torso, suddenly shrunk, the buttons popping like corn. It was good not to be hungry, but better still to be well-fed and corpulent, like an ancient Roman senator or an American aristocrat. Forgetting about the old adage, *Fill the belly and the eye will be ashamed,* he proudly patted his stomach and burped. An easy feeling, albeit momentary, washed over him, and was made all the more gratifying by the awareness that the feeling wouldn't last. By no means had he rid himself of that insidious thing, the undiagnosed condition with the insufferable incubation period. It was still skulking along the moors and fens of his mind, but as for now all was right in the world. Using his pinkie as a toothpick, he dug at the morsel of pork caught between his upper incisors. *Good meat this*, was the only thought swimming around in the vast ocean of his head. He listened absentmindedly to the jubilant song of the yellow-breasted warbler in the rose-garden out back and marveled at his own shadow growing dim as clouds herded passed the sun. Then, like a wild, solitary animal resting in a clearing, sensing that it was being watched (if only by God and the great trees in the dark and mossy woods), he startled and went lumbering oafishly through the house, buckling floorboards underfoot.

"*¡Vieja!*" he yelped, meaning his mother, borrowing the term of endearment from his father. "*¿Dónde andas?*"

He sniffed the rarified, barrio air, hoping that his prodigious nose would do what his ordinary eyes could not. Heightened by the yearning to see his mother, it smelled everything, every scent roiling around this little eastside borough, wave after heady wave: effluvia, the dirty diaper on the ass of the crying baby next door, the stench of something that had died, a decomposing cat lying in a gutter, maggots writhing in its smashed skull, killed by a speeding car three days ago near Hollenbeck Middle School, and everywhere there was the slightest hint of dearth; fragrant aromas, too, a whiff of sweet, Mexican bread wafting straight from the hot, brick ovens of *La Estrella* bakery on Soto Street, wisps of rose-scented, votive candle smoke laced with prayers, trailing from the sanctified alter of Saint Mary's Church and, dangling lightly there, the distinctive whiff of motherhood—not the motherhood of lactating breasts and maternal, honey breath wafting in the tiny nostrils of a new born son, as its mother sang him ancestral cradle hymns and whispered promises of a good and prosperous life. That time had

143

passed. This was motherhood in its waning days, that of an aging woman who had survived the birth of two cesarean sons, who had suffered when they suffered, and had sacrificed herself to ready them for the world (in her own, humble opinion she'd done a fine job, though lately she felt a tenuous sort of pride about it). Now this good woman had become the old, dignified matron of an endangered clan, and it was a thankless lot, redolent of overripe fruit.

"*Vieja*," he crooned, faithfully following his mighty nose. The great pining to see his mother was very much like the condemned man's last wish. Juan had to see her again or risk eternity in search of her, moaning ghostly woes, forever lamenting the things left unresolved, the things left unsaid. Luckily, he found her exactly where his nose led him, out on the sun-doused porch, in her snow-white smock and French-braided hair. She was sweeping the dust and cobwebs from behind the potted petunias and from beneath the white-washed, deacon's bench, the broom half-a-foot taller than her and a whole pound heavier. Still, she wielded it with freakish vigor, in swift, choppy strokes and quick, broad strokes. So fast that the act turned into a hazy dervish of dancing feet, straw and billowing, white twill.

If he had waited for her to acknowledge him he would've turned to dust, only to be swept into a dust-pan by his very own mother. Lamentably, he didn't have time for a slow death, no time now for the great dawdling called Life. In an attempt to draw her attention, Juan cleared his throat noisily and heaved a heavy sigh. And still she wouldn't look at him. Finally, he said:

"*Mamá, me voy,*" meaning to say: *Mamá, me voy a matar.*

"*Aye,*" she said, without looking at him. "*Qué te vaya bien.*"

144

That his own mother apparently wanted nothing to do with him, that she was treating him as if he were a common stranger or worse still a presumptuous suitor, baffled him and hurt him in a way that only she understood and sanctioned. The worst of it was that he didn't know why. A thousand likely reasons, like a thousand, unstoppable trains screeching into the night, going nowhere, ran in tandem through his head. Had he forgotten to thank her for the fine breakfast of pinto beans and hot corn tortillas yesterday morning? Had he not shown her sufficient gratitude for the oversized wardrobe lent to him last night?

The engines blew telling little puffs of smoke and shrieked: *No! Heavier things!* Veering abruptly, his mind went down a different set of tracks.

Did she begrudge him his birth, twenty-two years after the fact, because his life hadn't turned out like she planned? Or was she livid because she knew what he was about to do and that salvation, elusive as it was, would now be unattainable?

Say something *Mamá,* he nearly cried out. Talk to me like you know me, talk to me like faithful mothers talk to faithless sons on the day that they go away; say goodbye *Mamá,* because it's time for me to go; not back to that sad existence as a nameless student at the prominent university forty miles west of here, nor to any other harsh reality or state of mind in this world; none of this *Myself am Hell* shit. I'll go to *hell* and stay there for good.

He wanted to say all of these things to her and more, because he thought that it might make his untimely and tragic passing a little easier for the both of them. But her silence rendered his tongue impotent, so he couldn't even utter the meaningless, monosyllabic, "Umph, uh-uh!" of a deaf mute.

What he hadn't seen was his mother's solemn face, turned slightly away just then, streaming marble-size teardrops, her eyes closed tightly to protect them against the sun and the insufferable sight of a son's final departure, her lips atremble like a frightened butterfly caught in a spider's web, vainly fluttering its wings, muttering silent, devotional prayers, unbroken lyrical strings of Hail Marys, Our Fathers, *Gloria Patris* and *Salve Mi Hijo Diosito Mío!* It was the only thing she could do to stop it from happening.

Quietly, Juan stepped off of the porch and, without looking back, started walking, trying to put as much distance between himself and that woman as possible. He walked fast, to the rhythm of his own heart, thinking:

That's the thing about going away, if you're gone too long people stop missing you. Sooner or later they stop giving a shit if you come back or not, or if you live or die.

It was an unusually hot, spring morning in Boyle Heights, even for a boy born and raised in the Lower East Side of the city, far inland, boxed in by the Los Angeles River and the ugly, concrete maze of intersecting freeways. Too hot for anyone living amid the modern-day ruins of urban sprawl and the ubiquitous pall of photochemical smog, completely cut off from the Westside and the fresh, Pacific Ocean air. So hot that it wasn't yet nine o'clock and already Juan had broken into a heavy sweat. And yet he refused to walk in the shade, beneath the row of colossal, arching palms on the southside of Inez Street. In his last hours, he wanted only to walk in the sun.

Treading ever so lightly to keep from cracking the sidewalks, he moved steadily up the street. Marching along in his old army

146

boots, his heavy footfall sounded like the hoofed clomping of some mythical, sylvan creature.

"They call me *El Chivo of the Flats*," he mused. "Good morning! Clop-clop-clop! I've come to raise the dead! Clop-clop-clop! Time to wake-up! Clop-clop-clop!"

The neighbors, lying in their beds, opened their big, brown eyes and wondered:

"¡Qué chingado es ese ruido!"

They went to their windows and, against the better judgment of their frightened, whimpering children, peeled back the curtains in time to catch a glimpse of Juan lurching down the street. *"Ah,"* came a communal sigh, *"it's only the college educated Chicano kid who went cuckoo. He's a vato loco in the truest sense of the word. Common little bird."*

Too common these days, and yet he was a rare sort of winged thing, a Mexican starling with broken wings, broken spirit and broken mind, the first and last of his kind, an endangered species; not because he wasn't strong, intelligent or responsive to change. He had simply chosen self-extinction. Or rather, *something* had chosen it for him.

Stopping on the corner of Inez and Breed Street, he listened. Like a lover of Nature in the great outdoors, he listened. The streets fell silent and the tenement buildings and turn-of-the-century homes, awash in sparkling, April sunlight, sat as quietly as well-behaved school children. So quiet that he could hear a hushed, benevolent voice in the wind-nudged leaves, twittering on the still-green shoots of a little sapling. It was the Perpetual Monologue, sharing personal, ancient memories that were not his own, vivid glimpses of the past, the chronicles of Boyle Heights and all of its people.

This land, from Pleasant Avenue all the way to the Pomona Freeway, was once a lush and fertile vineyard where Mr. Boyle, the vine grower, grew fat, red grapes for table wine. Grapes grew abundantly, as did the population, as if he'd sown buckets of semen in the rich, black soil along with the grape seed. Up from the good earth they sprung, dark, primordial, genderless figures, caked in unctuous farmland muck, all teeming with horseflies, looking beastly enough. But beneath that crust of wet sod were the fair, blue-eyed, perfectly-pearly white sons and daughters of Shem. They settled in Las Viñas de Paredón Blanco, built houses, raised families, toiled and prospered. And a happy little lot of Shems they were. All of their days were without want. Their lives were good lives, and light the years between.

Then came the last days of Mr. Boyle. Old age and chronic illness tripped him up by the heels, and while he was down Death whispered in his ear, it's time to go now, Sir. You've had your moment in the sun. And he, knowing that it was in fact his time to go, nodded, agreeing to the terms. Yes, he said, I'll go, I'll go. Let me lay down.

Some men lay down to die in the middle of July, the Southwestern desert their thorny bed, among the dusty jaw-bones of lost cattle and the skulls of dead immigrants; others on frozen, mountain slopes just above the snow-line, on cold, godless, country nights, and still others within the dim and sterile confines of solitary hospice rooms while the nurse is out sneaking a cigarette. Mr. Boyle's was a king-sized, goose feather death-bed on a sturdy brass frame, capped by a bright, red silk canopy. And in his cloistered parlor (he had the servants move his bed into the parlor because it was the biggest and brightest room in the house) were all of the things which, collectively, composed the formal and dignified stages of this man's death—fields of sky-blue chrysanthemums (like the ones he'd seen in the colossal greenhouse at

148

the San Francisco World's Fair of 1915), a big mahogany, apothecary box brimming with every sort of elixir known to man, his private physician, all of his loved ones and, of course, the celestial hierarchy, the lot of them dangling overhead like shiny Christmas ornaments.

Lying there, in the final moments of his long and prosperous life, he lapsed in and out of consciousness. And then at last it came, a slow and uneventful passing, unlike anything he'd imagined while he had breath in his lungs or thoughts in his head or a glimmer in his eye. A simple gesture, really. He let go of the reins, handed them over to the Good Coachman. And gasping his last, he flip-flopped like a mackerel on the sweat-drenched sheets and babbled something about foreigners and the peopling of the world.

Fever dreams, said the doctor, trying his best to console the family. But deep down inside of Mr. Boyle's unconscious mind were fantastic, prophetic visions, in anticipation of the coming, or rather the return, of the sons and daughters of Ham.

As he stood there listening to the voice, staring skyward with mouth agape in awe, a street-sweeper whooshed passed, cut the curb too close and splashed cold, filthy gutter water in Juan's face. Coming quickly out of the state of mind that he was in, he spit up slop and a litany of Spanish and English curses, while the bemused driver smirked and waved to him in the side-view mirror. The slow-moving machine, equally unapologetic, went humming right along, its multiple nozzles spraying foamy white liquid, its huge, cylindrical, rear-end brush rotating like a paddle wheel. It left a broad, slick path in its wake, like a giant, orange snail trailing slime.

"Up your ass!" Juan shouted.

The street-sweeper's motor rumbled and in it was a retort: Go straight to hell boy!

"Yes," he said. "To hell I'll go so that my people won't have to."

He marched silently up Breed Street, listening carefully for the voice again. And there it was still, in the mute buzzing of the frayed telephone wires high above his head, barely a hum, yet clear as the sound of a golden flute. It picked up where it had left off before the disconnection.

Up from the good earth they sprung, dark, primordial, genderless figures, caked in the unctuous muck of uprising, uprooting and diaspora, teeming with horseflies, looking beastly enough. But beneath it were the beautiful, brown-eyed, perfectly bronzed sons and daughters of Ham, weeping like lost children of God, sobbing to themselves, To leave one's land is to suffer!

They settled in the land of the White Bluffs, rented rooms, raised families, toiled, and rarely prospered. And a tired bunch of Hams they were. All of their days were days of dearth. Their lives were hard, and dark the years between. But in spite of it all, or perhaps because of it, they multiplied, two-fold, ten-fold, one-hundred-fold, until there were so many of them that this land was deemed hopelessly heterogeneous by white men in government. So, the sons and daughters of Shem fled, abandoned their paradisiacal homeland, Las Viñas de Paredón Blanco, and sought refuge in the hills West of Boyle Heights. They were like an ad-hoc army, fighting an imaginary war, beating a glorious retreat from the field of battle while declaring victory, secretly incensed at having surrendered territory to an enemy which they deemed inferior.

O' but the days would come when the glorious sons and daughters of Shem would once again assert their dominion over all of the wild beasts, and a people they considered lower than wild beasts. Vexed by the memory of the things allegedly lost to Ham's kin, and bolstered by their inerrant right to object, they'd call for the heads of their enemies, call for wholesale deportations,

150

repatriations, anti-Ham laws and the like, so that Ham's children would dwindle in numbers and vanish from the shameful face of the earth. Yet in the morning, the sons and daughters of Ham would spring up from the good earth once again, indomitable as the grass of the field. And in spite of it all, or perhaps because of it, they'd become a nation, great, strong and numerous.

"So then," said Juan, determined not to change his mind, "what harm is there in killing myself. What's one less son of Ham?"

Against the Perpetual Monologue and the historical imperative, he rushed, fully expecting to be chided and beaten for his rebellion. That is unless he denied their sovereignty first, declaring: *This man, born in the year of our Redemption 19— is free! This life and this soul belongs to no one but me! I'm free to do as I will, without fear of retribution! I have the right to die as I choose. What's more, the past is prelude to absolutely nothing!*

Taking unduly pride in this unsubstantiated fact, he puffed up his chest and sidled down the street like a young boxer, a number one contender; and as sure footed a fellow as this one the world had never seen. He didn't know where he was going, but was cocksure of what he'd do once he got there. To the corner and west on Fourth Street, not counting his steps now, as he had as a boy while walking through the neighborhood. He was looking ahead, planning his next move, because up there, just beyond the biggest oak he'd ever seen in his life, awaited his last opponent, dwarfing the mighty oak itself, making it look like a miniature, green plastic tree. It would take him exactly three-hundred and sixty-six paces to get passed that juggernaut: Saint Mary's Parish and the last remnants of a Catholic boy's sense of guilt.

Eight o'clock mass was letting out, a saintly legion of little old Mexican ladies shuffling out of the church with their diminutive, hatted husbands hobbling after. Closer to the Almighty for having paid Him a visit, they said their goodbyes on the sidewalk, mumbled silent prayers as they left His house. They had lived long enough to memorize more prayers than the young, parish priest, more, in fact, than the parish's old monsignor himself. Drawing them piecemeal from a limitless and mysterious source, they could spout one for every earthly need or predicament. Morning prayers, mid-day prayers, and night time prayers. Prayers for the living, for longevity and for the dead; for love and for family, for health and fertility, for women wanting to bear children, for the birth pains of labor and for new born babies, for the sick and the suffering, for the afflicted, for the weary and for a happy death. And more would flow forth, least the well run dry. There were prayers against the loss of milk by nursing mothers, against human maladies and wild animals; against broken bones and bubonic plague; against mad dogs and lions; against sadness and loneliness, alcoholism, frenzy, mental illness and against sudden, tragic death. Prayers for suicides, too, but the hope was that any lost soul would heed the edict against attempting one's own life, the one that read like something straight out of a legal contract:

He has given man operative dominion of life, the right to use it and preserve it, as the occupant of a house is bound to take good care of it. Therefore, suicide goes against the dominion of God's ownership and shall be deemed a violation to His rights.

Of course he knew the decree by heart, could recite it in his sleep, in his dreams, in languages which he didn't even know that he spoke. And so to willfully amend it, to assert the unspoken privilege of a squatter and claim, *I have dominion over my own life, and have the right to end it if I choose,* was tantamount to a coup d'

Dieu. The thought of civil engineers changing the course of a God-made river came to mind and made him smile. But on this day, these old church-goers had been charged with the task of making sure that he kept to the letter and the spirit of the law. They saw him coming and deliberately lingered longer than usual on the sidewalk outside of St. Mary's Church, determined not to let him cross the street and go about the grim business of doing himself in. He would have to go through them, brave the ranks of these seasoned Christian soldiers, obstinate one and all, none of whom believed in such a thing as a Lapsed Catholic. *Once a Catholic, always a Catholic*, was their creed. They'd fight to save him. In the name of the Father (who never stopped being a father to an ungrateful bunch of children), and the Son (who did everything he could to save them) and the Holy Ghost (the quiet, benevolent uncle who always believed that it was possible to save them), they'd knock him down so that he might rise again anew.

Into the ring he stepped, as the bells of Saint Mary's tolled the start of the bout, unprepared for the pangs of salvation, thinking, *¡Estos viejitos me van a romper la madre, pero no me queda remedio!*

Out of the corner of his eye he saw the first comer, fighting on behalf of the grand, heavyweight champion of all times. A gritty, squat-set, flat-nosed grandmother came rushing toward him like a screeching freight train, in a black satin veil, her finest Depression era dress and loose, nylon stockings. Her pudgy little fists at the ready, she came in close, wanting to pummel him until he saw the error of his ways, until he begged for sweet mercy, crying out, "God save me!" But he slipped passed her in one spry motion and left her standing there, hunkered over, furiously gasping for breath.

"*¡Cobarde!*" she shouted after him.

"No more than any other man in this world," said Juan.

"*¡Vete al Diablo!*" she yelled.

"*Acompáñame,*" he said, edging along the curbside.

Then another comer, four foot ten, weighing in at one-hundred six pounds (with cane), a toothless, lean, leathery old gentleman in shirt sleeves, suspenders and a dusty, chocolate brown Derby. He drew near, sucking incessantly at his gums, and let loose a torrent of blows—left jabs, straight rights, hooks and upper cuts—surprisingly agile for a man his age. He was aiming for the young man's colossal nose, an easy enough target, or so he thought.

"I'm going to smash in that ugly sinner's beak of yours," said the old man, "and make you bleed the Blood of the Lamb!"

Parrying to the left and to the right, Juan dodged those arthritic fists, and so the only thing that the old man hit was the hot, stagnant air.

"Is that all you got old man?" Juan taunted.

"Stand and fight *¡cabrón!*" said the old man.

"Some other time," he said. "I don't want to be late to my own funeral."

"Yes, and after the funeral," said the old man, "go down. He'll be waiting for you there."

As if to show how swiftly the soul would descend, the old man made an odd, vulgar, downward gesture with his wiry hands and whistled long and low. But Juan, entirely convinced that the fight was won, pumped his fist triumphantly in the air, let down his guard and started a slow retreat toward Hollenbeck Park. He didn't even see what hit him, only felt a blinding hot wallop and a

154

sudden loss of his senses as it caught him squarely on the chin and sent him flying against invisible ropes.

"¡Es un pecado joven!" said a livid little voice, like an angel or a devil on the shoulder. *"Y cuando la soga aprieta, derechito al infierno."*

His vision blurry from the blow, he looked back in awe at his assailant, wondering what kind of a bruiser he was up against. And there she was, in the half-light of the sun and the shadow of the church, a waiflike great-grandmother, mighty as love, a curly strand of silver hair looping out from beneath a dun-colored veil, her face an ancient mosaic of dark, cancerous sun-spots, hairy moles, and wrinkles that told of a life time of silent submission, servitude and sorrow.

She's spiteful because you're going to get out of this life while you're young, he told himself. *She's taking it out on you, the bitter old Nana! That was just a love tap. She's going to take your head off. Move your feet! Get clear of her! Move or risk being saved!*

He shook it off, regained his footing and, perhaps pitied by the one he meant to defy, managed to backpedal out of the old woman's reach as the bells of Saint Mary tolled a ninth time, signaling the end of the match. *Nine o'clock,* he thought, wiping sweat from his forehead. *The old folks slowed me down. I should have been dead by now.*

Out of sheer habit, he went to make the sign of the cross, but caught himself in the act and quickly repressed the impulse, smothering one hand in the palm of the other. And with it the urge to look back at Saint Mary's Parish one last time. He pressed on, hastening toward the park and a speedy and inevitable death, recalling an old Catholic hymn about hell, thinking, *O' Death! O' Judgment! O' blazing fires! O' forever! O' fuck it!*

155

12

Hollenbeck Park was never meant to be a park. The land itself, twenty-one odd acres just east of the river, could easily have been a private golf course or a sprawling estate, complete with tennis courts, sparkling swimming pools, thoroughbred stables and dozens of Mexican servants. Instead it had been donated, for ornament and recreation, to the public by Mr. Hollenbeck's widow and the city mayor. Yet the real reason for their generosity was not known. The romantic-naturalist would argue that it was so that the beauty of nature might prevail. The wealthy friends of the benefactors would proudly say that it was a philanthropic gesture in the grand style of the first American tycoons, while critics thought it a cheap, political ploy to win new constituents or perhaps to attract desirable residents and investors. Juan himself believed that the park was here to serve a more practical purpose. It would be his final resting place, because at this silent hour, with the otherworldly, gossamer-veil of sunlight draped softly over the bright green lawns, the rolling, woody knolls and the still waters of the man-made lake, it looked like a cemetery.

He walked down to the edge of the misty, thumb-shaped lake and rested awhile beneath three black poplars, which nature had grafted together by the branches and roots. The trees were positioned just so, like three, young, smiling brothers in their finest

Sunday suits, posing for a sibling portrait.

This must be the place, he thought, at peace for once in his life. All quiet and serene, he sprawled out dreamless against the poplars, his body as empty as a universe without light or divinity. He breathed in the heat of the day and the phosphorescent dust which fell in mysterious abundance from the sky, breathed it all in and held it. Bottled up in his lungs, the glowing specks drifted about randomly in darkness, moved across the expanse of twin air sacs, floated passed one another without ever touching. But after a time, and purely by chance, the dust gravitated toward the center and, like incendiary atoms, fused, ignited and came alive in original form. He held his breath, longer than humanly possible. All was in suspense, all was calm and silent. Nothing existed. And then he exhaled.

A thing called Light appeared blindingly in a place called Sky. A new earth sprouted fresh spring grass, the cypress and pines put forth new shoots, the lake was suddenly thick with fish and the air abounded with every sort of song bird. Life had come to Hollenbeck Park, and he had come with it, if only to stay for a short while, only until the grand, mysterious scheme to end his own life crystallized in his mind and became a reality.

Rising unsteadily to his feet, he gazed into the dark, green waters of the lake, saw faint, reoccurring images of himself in the ripples. It was good to exist in this new creation, where to kill oneself was not a sin, where it was actually the moral thing to do.

Go forth and perish, something inside of him insisted.

The new marching orders, though anticipated, came down surprisingly hard and sudden—an impetuous command from a foolish, hilltop general to a lowly foot soldier. Still, there were strange assurances in what was to him every dying man's rationale. He'd heard multiple versions of this logic, most recently in the cinema—a tragic Dutch film about a Christian woman who falls in love with an atheist. In the closing scene, the nonbeliever kills himself by jumping in front of oncoming traffic. He is run over by a big, black Cadillac, the unrepentant driver a priest drunk on holy wine. And as the atheist lay dying in the middle of the road, coughing up blood, he whispered to the night and to his absent lover:

"Yes, Charlotte, you were right. Death ends life, but death ends death, too, and the worrying of it."

These words resonated in his heart now, on his ending day, making his fate a little easier to swallow.

"I understand," he said. "And I will comply."

With this he set out to find death, playing a morbid kind of hide-and-go-seek, wondering with childlike whimsy, *where o' where is death? Is it crouching pixie-like behind the willows on the hill, snickering into its cold white hands to muffle its melancholy glee? Or is it lurking like a strangler in the lakeside ramada, out to murder a man in broad daylight? Or sitting right in front of me, in the tall grass, indifferent as a government clerk, waiting to punch my card and send me on my way? O' where is death? Ollie Ollie oxen free!*

Around the lake, a mile or so, wound a narrow, concrete footpath, which he would follow to its end or to his own, whichever came first. As far as he could see, clear across the idyllic length and breadth of water, land and sky, all the way to South Boyle Avenue, there were no people in the park, not a living soul. A twinge of macabre delight shot up his spine, making him skip a way down the path.

"Nobody is going to save you," he said, looking up with a nervous little grin.

In time to a silent funeral dirge he marched, passed the little, whitewashed bandstand that sat among the palms on the grassy slope. In and around that century-old structure lingered a host of lost spirits, all of them clinging to a familiar, comforting memory of a perfect, Sunday afternoon spent at Hollenbeck Park. He couldn't see them, couldn't see the delicate imprint of their faces in the hot, transcendent air, couldn't hear them either, the low prattle of invisible tongues (the dead gossip too). Yet they were all there, up on the empty, dilapidated stage: a debonair, 1940s crooner in mid-high note, his arms outstretched to a modest-sized audience of young, well-dressed *pachucos* with their pomaded pompadours and their pretty, ruby-lipped, high-coifed haired *rucas*. They turned their heads in unison as he walked passed and started rumors about him, which just happened to be true.

They say he's messed up in the head.

Crazier than Chato's big brother, who used to strut up and down Brooklyn Avenue at midnight, talking to strangers, stray dogs and angels, the one who got committed to the psych ward of the Santa Fe Railroad Hospital in 33' and ended up jumping out of a third story window. They say his head came apart like a pomegranate when he hit the ground.

I heard different.

What'd you hear?

I heard that he isn't crazy at all, that he only thinks he is.

So why does he want to kill himself.

He doesn't want to kill himself.

Then why did he come to Hollenbeck Park today?

He came to talk himself out of death; he's looking for a reason to live.

159

There is no reason to live.

He thought that he heard voices coming from the bandstand, but when he turned to look there was nobody there.

Wind in the palms, he mused, pressing on without giving it another thought.

When he reached the lake bridge, he stopped for a moment to examine traces of waterfowl—fossilized droppings and frayed feathers. They were everywhere, all along the high, concrete banks of the lake, in the pristine blades of grass, on the park benches and along the footpath, but there were no ducks. He surveyed the water and the sky, and scratched his head.

Funny, he thought, *no ducks, didn't I make ducks when I made the lake, and the park, and the world?*

An oversight perhaps. He couldn't recall. But there, lying at his feet, was what looked like an abandoned duck egg—smooth, cream-colored and speckled. He hesitated to pick it up, not wanting to disrupt the natural order of things. But curiosity got the better of him and he quickly snatched it off the ground.

Right away he knew that he'd been duped. Nature had played a harmless prank on him. It wasn't an egg at all, but an ovoid stone—shiny, flat and lightweight. He held it gently in the palm of his hand, as if it were fragile.

Good one, he thought, looking skyward with a wry grin.

Not quite angry or amused, he stared at the stone and labored to push unnatural laughter from his lungs, which finally came out sounding like a pack of wild, braying donkeys. As if to purge his psyche of this half-ass, cosmic joke, he flung the stone the length of the lake. It skipped elegantly along the mirror-surface, six times, passed the little, one-tree island, and sank.

How beautifully it sank, he noted.

Yes, how lovely it sank, gurgled a chorus of caterwauls from the depths of the lake.

"Who said that," he demanded, edging closer to the banks.

The answer came at once, air bubbles and bright flaxen eyes rising from the bottom to the murky green waterline. Up came reptilian snouts, scaly heads and broad, stony shells—a bale of primordial, turtlesque creatures. *Chanes,* or so his mother used to call them. Water spirits who lay in wait on the banks of ponds, rivers and lakes to steal wayward children.

Don't go, they pleaded, *stay here with us, come into the water, let us see you.*

"What do you want?" he asked.

We want only to see you, beautiful boy, they assured him, *come into the water.*

In his short stint as an English major at the university, he'd yet to hear such poetry. It was not the sentimental, self-indulgent language of Shakespearean sonnets, but the true voice of heartbroken lovers; and he was the sole object of their affection. To his ears it sounded like, "We have been waiting for you all of our lives!" Something *wanted* him, the things in the lake *wanted* him, the mythical, pre-Cuauhtémoc turtle-gods floating in the shallows, and death swirling florescent and nebulous in the algae, *wanted* him.

Aglow in soft, warm, transcendent happiness, he inched closer to the water, ignoring the warning sign posted to the dying palm tree which read:

NO WADING OR SWIMMING.

Were he an expert swimmer, he might have bound his legs together with sailor's rope to avoid the instinct of self-preservation.

161

But he didn't bother with this small detail because he couldn't swim a stroke.

This is it, he told himself. *I will go into the lake and the lake will go into me, until all consciousness is lost, until my blessed, brown skin turns a distinctive, lifeless shade of white, as I sink silently to the bottom, the end, yours truly, Juan Juárez Bitol.*

He imagined the story of his death in the morning papers:

A fisherman discovered the body of an unidentified, young Hispanic male floating in Hollenbeck Lake early Tuesday morning. The official cause of death is yet to be determined, but all indications point to suicide by drowning.

As he daydreamed by the lake, his mother was pruning her roses in the garden of the house on Inez Street, de-thorning every stem on the bush and every thorny fact in the yet-to-be written article, imagining a different ending to the newspaper story, good news, a miracle.

A young, unidentified, Hispanic male nearly drowned in Hollenbeck Lake yesterday morning. Authorities say that as he was being lured into the water by strange voices, his loving mother, Doña Guadalupe, 63 of Boyle Heights, saved his life by calling out to him:

"Come on, don't stop. Come on! Don't go into the water. Keep walking."

He heard her unspoken sentiments clearly, a palpable signal transmitting straight to his heart by way of the mysterious, telegraphic line between mother and son. Despite his assumption that she didn't care what happened to him, she hadn't lost hope that he could be saved, and this message translated into a stay of execution. Whether or not he liked it, he could not drown himself in the lake. His mother's prayers precluded it. Still, his sudden retreat from the water's edge could not have been considered an act of volition. With a truculent grunt he walked away, even as the *Chanes* wept, their cavernous nostrils bubbling snot, their sad, bovine eyes flooding with tears.

O' don't go dear boy! they moaned. *Come into the water!*

"I have to go now," he said.

Gjirlp! Hulpr-pupu-uu! Awwwa! they howled, imitating deep, human sorrow.

One by one the turtle-gods dove down to the deep end of Hollenbeck Lake, their little air bubbles bursting softly on the surface, emitting unearthly, garbled sobs. They returned to where they had come from, to the seldom read, back-pages of Mexican folklore, and to the dark nooks in the minds of little Mexican children.

He walked on, seemingly having resigned himself to living a prolonged life with mental illness. Yet beyond the façade of acquiescence, he was cursing the lost opportunity. It was only old wisdom with a new, grim twist that lightened his spirits.

When the gallows are disabled, he concluded, *the sun gleams brightly on the guillotine.*

"Yes, plan *B* will do just fine," he said, taking heart and trudging on.

The bend in the path took him to an isolated spot at the far end of the park that he'd walked through on many occasions, but this time he came upon something he'd never seen before, and it put the fear of God into him. An outgrowth of rogue trees was pushing out beyond their circumscribed plot in the earth, their overarching canopy looming precariously overhead, blocking out the sun. Wild palms swayed in the otherwise still, morning air; weeping willow branches coiled and lashed out like tentacles, set on snatching up and devouring unsuspecting passersby; towering Lombardy poplars bellowed and flexed their burly trunks. Roots of mammoth girth and power tore loose from the soil and shattered the cement footpath under his trembling feet. He could feel a jungle heat coming off of the trees and the fiery sting of gnats on his neck.

These were not problematic trees, given free rein by the defeated landscaping crews of the department of parks and recreation. This was Nature—alive, furious and vengeful—taking back everything it had once lost to civilization, slowly, steadily creeping towards the so-called master planned, superhighway on the other side of the lake, intent on crushing the thousand-mile road, the mega-tons of rebar and concrete, like crêpe paper.

In the shadows of colossal trees and the upstart California Interstate 5 Freeway he cowered, bore silent witness to a battle that had been raging since civilization began, a conflict perceptible only to wild beasts and lunatics. He could not look away, nor could he plug his ears to muffle the sound of open warfare between these two opposing forces—on one side cars honking a call to arms, artillery firing in the shifting gears of diesel engines, the low rumble of concrete expanding in the heat of the day, as loud as the boots of an invading army marching on cobblestones; and on the other side was Nature, savage trees assaulting the forward position of the enemy with an eerie echo as a war cry.

"This *thing* can't go on forever," he said. "It's got to stop. It will stop, within the hour or by the end of the century. It's got to stop. Either way, I won't be here to see it."

Not quite ready to straddle the fine, perilous line between the indomitable forces of the natural world and the grand, but

164

ultimately ephemeral works of civilization and modern man, he took a few faltering steps forward. But in his haste, he didn't realize there was nowhere to go.

Up ahead, the park path took a sudden hairpin turn beneath the Golden State Freeway and directly into the hard, lifeless underside of the *thing* he was trying to escape, the *thing* not wholly responsible for his illness, but that had very well played a big part in it. This *thing,* crawling through the Boyle Heights landscape and the most scenic part of the park, had the look of a rare, sickly animal that should have been extinct a long time ago—a graceless, godless, artificial dinosaur; a pale-gray, twelve-legged flat-back creature, infested from head to tail with slow moving, four-wheeled, honking parasites.

Juan was rooting for the trees. Behind him, champion trees—the tallest, stoutest, and oldest in the city—had already taken the footpath, leaving no sign that it had existed and no way back. He waited, stranded on an island of his own making, not worrying about what would happen next. And all around him the world went on.

A sleek, black and white squad car cruised along Saint Louis Street, like a big jungle cat on the hunt. Ants in the grass worked hard to undo the damage done to their colony by an absent-minded, heavy-footed park-goer. A Boeing 747 jetliner flew overhead, came barreling down out of the clear blue sky at subsonic speed, so low in its flight pattern that it practically parted Juan's hair down the middle and left him temporarily deaf.

"*Pinche* jumbo!" he shouted after it, the taste of jet fuel lingering on his tongue.

As he stood there bad mouthing the commercial airline

industry and pilots, co-pilots and air-traffic controllers everywhere, waiting for his hearing to return, he spotted a big, fawn-colored falcon gliding slowly passed. It circled the park silently, numerous times, before its calls registered in his ears—a long, rising and falling of human-like cries and maniacal laughter. It swooped down low, its wingspan a full ten feet wide, and sailed gracefully along the surface of the lake, shot skyward toward the stratosphere and vanished into the sun. In its wake, its wild shrieks echoed, louder than the jetliner that had preceded it. It went on like this indefinitely, until at last he realized that he was the one laughing hysterically, not the falcon; until he became cognizant, with intense, yet tempered joy, that the squad car had pulled to the curb and that the policemen in it were watching him closely, as if he were about to perpetrate a great crime.

"Yes," he said, watching them in turn with joy. "My plan *B*."

Days past he wouldn't have greeted the officers with a smile, wouldn't have welcomed them as emissaries of a happy death. He would have taken to the hills, sought shelter in the grassy mounds of dirt surrounding the park, the earth the workers displaced when they dug the hole for the lake. A survival instinct, reminiscent of a cautionary childhood chant warning of *El Cucuy*, would have warned him, *Run, run, run away, live to be profiled another day*. His mind still housed implicit memories of the day the cops, the constables on patrol, *la chota o patrulla*, stopped poor Pablo as he rode his ten-speed bicycle home from work, because he looked suspicious riding his old Schwinn down sunny Sheridan Street. The drill was practically a ritual in this neighborhood, every word and silence, every motion and moment of immobility a time honored tradition by every player. First the cops: "Don't move! Let me see the hands!

166

Don't you fucking move," with their service revolvers drawn and pointed at Pablo. Forget the pepper spray, because a cop in Boston claimed that Hispanics were impervious to it because they ate a spicy diet. And Pablo, braking on command, the bike chain pulling so taut on the sprocket that it snapped in half. He did not move, did not speak, despite not having been read his Miranda Rights. Not because he feared self-incrimination. He just didn't want to get shot.

What Juan wanted, conversely, was for the two cops sitting in their black-and-white squad car to judge him to be a very viable threat and to have no choice but to gun him down in the gentle light of April, despite new life coming into Hollenbeck Park and into the world. It would be no great feat, he concluded. It wasn't like throwing rocks at a hornet's nest and waiting to be stung to death. All he had to do was walk in their direction and cast them a contemptuous look.

"I don't know if there is a God," said Juan. "I seriously doubt it. But if there is, I'm sure He sent them here for this one specific purpose. Today these men aren't devils. Today they're angels of mercy. Today these second-rate civil servants are first-rate killers."

These gentlemen, he thought distantly, wholly present and yet far away, *have come here today to witness the self-destruction of a sad and lonely man. They've come to end his life.*

Digressing further still, he thought, *Scientists even have a term for it, the cellular machinery of programmed cell death, yes, apoptosis!*

He saw them plainly, in panoramic view, through the windshield of their squad car, the typical pairing—the young lion and the old; the rookie fresh out of the academy, a little boy face and a dearly grown mustache, a clean conscience and a savior's complex; and the veteran, with a life time of service to the Department, passed his prime, not quite fit for duty, but still alive and, unlike his new partner, clean-shaven and not so clean of conscience. In the blooming light of day, he saw them for what they really were—stage-actors, understudies waiting to go on, born to play parts both comical and tragic: the first sons of civilization, minions of the law and occasionally, like today, unwitting assassins. They had a transparent, yet altogether unconscious look of pathos about them, the distinctive drawing down at the corners of the mouth, the dimming of the eyes, and the fallen brow.

It almost made Juan feel sorry for them, slouched blindly in their patrol unit with no likely way of knowing what was about to happen. He almost felt sorry for their wives and their children, who would suffer as the policemen suffered, during the three months of paid leave and the ongoing investigation, until at last an impartial arbitrator, prudent not to call it by any other name, would rule the shooting death of this young, Mexican-American college student a tragic case of victim-precipitated homicide. And then, like official state executioners, the officers would be granted a warrant protecting them against a charge of murder.

If there was justice, here on earth and up in heaven, he would not die today. Ah, but if he got lucky, these cops wouldn't be the Keystone kind, wouldn't slip on banana peels, fall on their asses and bungle the whole god damn thing.

Under the watchful gaze of the lawmen, and calm as Sunday morning, he walked briskly toward the squad car. He moved with the urgency of a man abandoning a burning house, the one he'd lived in all of his life, and yet he did not feel the slightest bit of nostalgia in his heart, did not feel homesick (a queer emotion after all); nor did he look back one last time. Forward, as the occasion permitted, watching with unremitting joy the policemen stirring from their late-shift stupor, frothing lightly at the mouth as they went for their guns. But it was the last thing that he saw, because the sun caught the officers' golden badges just so and the sunlight flashed in Juan's eyes and blinded him.

It was good, he thought, regarding his life, *it was good that it was.*

Waiting blindly and patiently for the fiery torrent of bullets that would lay him low and into the grave, he slipped gently into an unfamiliar state of being or rather *not-being*, one of warmth, weightlessness and great serenity; a return to a pre-embryonic stage before there was sensibility, cognition and the inevitable failing of mental health. Something inside of him, an impulse unlike thought, told him that this was what it was like to be dead. At first there was nothing, and beyond that nothing, and then, quite suddenly and unexpectedly, *nothing*. But then it corrected itself, claiming ignorance of death, because he was actually still alive.

"I'm *not* dead," he said.

The proof lay in his heart, still beating, and in his mind, still thinking, and in his soul, still anchored to his withered body by the slight weight of sapience, stupidity and a divine flicker of light. And if this wasn't enough to dispel all doubt that he was still alive, there was the sound of yet another jetliner sailing through the air. Like the first jetliner it flew too low, at landing elevation, the myopic pilots apparently having mistaken Juan's narrow back for an airport runway. With a piercing, sonic-whistle it came lumbering down toward the earth, a machine from the sky, a wide-bodied, double-deck behemoth. It was saying something to him as it flew overhead, something in an aeronautic tongue, in the language of aero-planes, not spelled out neatly like a Western Union telegram, but he understood it, was able to decipher the message in the spinning turbines. It sounded like an angry father's rant, cruel and unrelenting because, as he well knew, ignorant beasts do not respond to kindness.

¡Ay, pero como puedes ser tan pendejo! it bellowed. *¡Sálvate bruto! ¡Sálvate!*

A stone heavy hand slapped him square on the back of the head, knocked some sense into his Cro-Magnon skull and gave him back his sight. He could see again and for a moment stood blinking dumbly up at a big, flaming orb sinking slowly in the darkening sky, which turned out to be nothing but the setting sun. His gaze drifted downward, drew level, and there was the lake, serene as a late afternoon catnap when no one's looking, and the colossal Lombardy poplars, silent and still as in antiquity, as in a Grecian urn depicting a haunted forest. There, too, was the Golden State Freeway at rush hour, all stopped up with cars and trucks and shrouded in a dusty, brown haze of toxic emissions.

The day had gone. The cops had gone, too, off to another part of the city, responding to an emergency call, reports of a jaywalker dashing across North Cummings Street, a traffic signal light out on Orme Avenue, an abandoned bicycle found near Pomeroy Avenue.

What did he care? The involuntary feeling of wanting to live had taken a hold of him and wouldn't let go.

"Fine," he said, hoping to appease the feeling. "Tomorrow apparently does matter. I'll give it another shot, see if it doesn't get better."

170

Oh, but Juan was stubborn! Oh, how he spat and gnashed his teeth, skulking home in the gloaming, grumbling, "Yes, tomorrow matters, but only until tomorrow."

13

Up on Spangler Hill, just beyond the parking lot of Chadwick Hall, Juan squatted like a great ape behind an oak tree. He peered across the asphalt lot, watching them come and go. He had been waiting there since midday, after a grueling, three-hour, stop-and-go bus ride from Boyle Heights. He had been waiting there for a hundred winters, suffering well through rain and frost and the unexpected snowy nights not noted in the yellowing pages of any *Farmers' Almanac*. Squatting behind the same, knotted tree for centuries, through common years and leap years (gaining absolutely nothing by virtue of the days added to his life), he talked to himself, scratched his pumpkin-sized head and pondered the existence of a benevolent Being. He was alone and relatively happy. Then one day, he saw a small group of tall, blond men in straw hats ascending the hill, saw them standing breathless at the top of the hill, marveling at the expanse of rolling, green hills below the early morning mist. At first he was cautiously curious and crawled toward them on his belly, within a stone's throw, to get a better look at them. They were men like him, walked upright just like him, spoke a language (unlike his, but it was definitely a language of some sort), and presumably dreamt of the future (one which had already been determined by them). Men like Juan, if only in anatomy, because they were different in every other respect, as in the way they made grandiose gestures atop the hill, waving their hands freely across the virgin, Southern California landscape, marking their territory. When he saw them doing this, he chewed his claws down to the nubs, realizing that things were about to change and that he could do nothing to stop it. In those few hours spent atop the yet-to-be named hill, they had already completed their grand designs, had built their lofty structures and were inhabiting them.

What kind of men are these? he had asked, a question charged with panic and wonder. *What quick, crafty, minds?*

The tall, blond men in straw hats went away, but returned in three days' time in numbers, heading up trains of sweaty pack-mules weighed down with modern tools and tons of building materials—Günter chains, leveling instruments, tripods, boxes of saws and hammers, barrels of nails, cords of lumber, stone, brick and mortar, to survey the land, to build the university and the hall that stood before him. And unlike Rome, it *was* built in a day. As notice of their permanence, of their intention to stay for good, they parked their brand new, Model-T Fords in neat, little rows in the sun, in the dirt lot outside of the hall.

He was still squatting there, behind that same oak tree, sullied haunches set squarely on muddy heels, when their descendants came decades later, pulling up in their two-tone, twilight blue Plymouth convertibles, back from their springtime holidays on tropical islands, all golden tanned and happy, smelling of sweet coconut oil and playing beach music. Those days, the ones they would later remember as the happiest of their lives, came and went, ephemeral as dreams. And now those same students were returning as alumni, as proud mothers and fathers, double-parking their European sedans in the cul-de-sac out in front of Chadwick

Hall, unloading suitcases of all sizes, shopping bags, finely wrapped parcels and tennis rackets, saying goodbye to their sons and daughters, the fine young heirs of the university.

The hall lobby was a sea of sentimental faces—a father kissing his freshman daughter on the forehead, murmuring a personal message of affection into her ear, while slipping her a sheaf of crisp, new twenty dollar bills with a wink and a smile; a mother embracing her handsome young son, the engineering student, squeezing him tightly around the small of his back, not wanting to let him go, doing so only after he'd promised to phone home frequently.

It was love by proxy for Juan, out there beyond the parking lot, like a man staring at a distant bonfire, feeling no warmth, comforted only by the memory of fire. He looked on, shivering in the cold mud, lost in the fog of his own seclusion. The night came on and the stars took to the sky. The great, high hall lit up floor-by-floor as the students settled comfortably into their dorm-rooms for a quiet evening of study and social drinking. And still Juan waited, until the lights went out and every window glazed over black, and every student nestled into their bed. Only then did he emerge from behind the oak tree, lumber across the darkened lot, up the steps and right through the front doors of Chadwick Hall.

The lobby, the cordial greeter of all those who came to the hall, did not welcome him when he stepped foot inside. The rich, red carpet and soft, ochre armchairs and fine façonné drapery did not welcome him, indeed wanted nothing to do with him. There was music playing, too, the eclectic selections of college radio, unreleased B-sides and florid, Martian songs, playing for all of the

174

poor insomniacs, for the potheads and the handful of dedicated undergrads pulling all-nighters, but not for him. The twelve golden notes, strung together just so to make those melodies, broke apart, becoming a fragmented drone in his ears.

"Ha!" he cried out, half a guffaw for a cruel joke that had lost all sense of cosmic irony. It was getting old, this unspoken bias. Beyond old really, it was absurd and archaic and he wished that it would stop. But even at the tender age of twenty-two years, he realized that to wish death upon something so ancient, something which had existed since the convergence of the Tribes of Men, and had survived in the heart of humankind throughout reoccurring ages of darkness and enlightenment, was pure folly. It was alive and well, still running in the veins of men and institutions, in the cities, out in the country and everywhere in between. It wore many masks and went by a thousand different names. Sometimes it was inclement weather, a dark cloud following him around campus, into lecture halls and down into the Village, pouring cold buckets of rainwater on him while the sun shone brightly on every other head. Other times it was English professors who wittingly or unwittingly made insensitive remarks during lecture and, in doing so, banished him to the hinterlands along with all of those fictitious monsters and villains in the Western literary canon. Now it was Chadwick Hall itself, which he had called home for the past five years, that was keeping him out in the cold and darkness, beyond the parking lot, hiding behind an oak tree.

He went in just the same, used the lavish, French drapes to wipe the sticky, pine needles and grime from his hands and stomped across the thick, burgundy carpet, purposely leaving a trail of muddy boot prints as a sign that he existed, that he had been here. In the morning, someone—a beautiful, if slightly melodramatic, blond coed from the Valley or an oversensitive residential counselor or the dumb-struck day clerk—would come across the clods of dirt that were Juan's tracks and remark with an air of utter repugnance, *What kind of an animal would do this?* But it wouldn't matter to him, because as far as he was concerned they'd been talking about him since the day he arrived at the university. He couldn't prove it, but neither could they deny it.

Pushing on through the lobby, he came upon the night-clerk, a student on the work-study program who presently was doing neither, having fallen asleep on the job. Behind him, the rows of student mailboxes lay empty, which must have justified, at least in the night-clerk's tired mind, taking a short nap. His head was buried deep in a textbook on entomology, his cheeks pink, sweaty and luminous. A fresh speck of hot spit glistened on his chin and the pages of the book, like the monarch butterflies in the glossy photos therein, fluttered lightly under the gentle current of his breathing. Above his silky, flaxen locks, an Act of Parliament clock on the wall was telling Juan that the sun would be rising in a few hours, but he ignored it and drew closer to the front counter to watch the night-clerk sleep. He was drawn to him, thrilled by the veiled danger of observing such a seemingly uneventful act. It was like the time as a boy when his father persuaded him to pose for a photograph with a lion in a traveling menagerie of wild animals at the Los Angeles County Fair. The poor, big cat was lying under a raggedy, candy-striped tent, sprawled out atop a filthy bed of straw, its tongue hanging out of its ponderous maw. It was shackled and tranquilized, of course, had probably been de-clawed as well, but it didn't keep Juan from feeling exhilarated, thinking—

You can't hurt me Mr. Lion, thinking, with still a healthy sense of God-given prudence, *Oh, but please don't wake up and eat me Mr. Lion!* He did not fear the night-clerk either, at least not while he slept, and so he stood there and stared boldly at him. At that moment, he actually *loved* the night-clerk in all his whiteness, loved his rich, Anglo-Saxon blood, his light blue eyes and perfectly shaped nose. He loved him like a brother, because at the moment he could do Juan no harm.

"Sleep well, Brother John," he said.

The night-clerk stirred, his snores rattled in his throat and he mumbled something in a garbled dream language, a sound like an old motorcycle being kick-started. But Juan was thoroughly convinced that the night-clerk was actually trying to communicate something of great importance to him. You could see a solemn urgency on his face, slightly disfigured though it was by the weight of his head pressing down upon it. He leaned in closer to listen, smiling in anticipation of having a nice, friendly chat with the night-clerk. It was part of the American college experience after all, wasn't it? Getting to know new people, making connections like nerve impulses across synapses, networking, making lifelong friendships? This was, for him, the great, improbable leap over the junction gap, over the chasm of racial divide. He was being addressed by a white classmate and had the common courtesy to reply. He was trying hard to be social, to make a connection, to make an acquaintance, maybe even a friend.

"What was that you said, Brother John?" he asked

"Kuj-quxr-gwj," the night-clerk murmured.

"Yes, I am a student at this university."

"Puk butz, jur-tzt."

"Yes, I live in this hall. I got a dorm-room downstairs, right next to the boiler-room. You'd be surprised how quiet it is down there. It's like living at the bottom of the Pacific Ocean. I've got the whole floor to myself, too. I've got a private toilet and an asphalt view of the parking lot through a transom window. And I only pay half of what the other students pay. If you don't mind the occasional rat or leaky pipes overhead or the angry ghosts of Chadwick Hall who shriek at midnight, or the solitude, it's perfect shelter. Tell me, do you think you'd like living *down there*? What I mean to say is, do you think you could?"

The night-clerk turned his head, drooled and grunted: *"Speq, bilj ruz speq."*

"What did you say to *me*?" asked Juan.

It was not like him to get upset, to make a public spectacle and draw attention to himself. He had survived this long at the university by practicing the old ways, the old quietism, by lowering his head, tucking his tail and keeping silent in the ugly face of not-so-subtle racial slurs. But with the barb still fresh in his side and his dignity bleeding out, he had to say something in his own defense and in the name of all of those who would not speak up. If he let it go unanswered, he would startle from unsettling dreams one night, years after the fact, with a bold and witty retort on his tongue that came too late, jabbering on about how God had made him, too, about how he was a man and not a cockroach, and how he had a brain, a backbone, balls and a soul to prove it. If he kept quiet this time, he would look back one gray, dismal day and the shame of it all would swallow him alive. He had to say something. Admissions of guilt and apologies were in order! Donning the glorious cloak of a latter-day champion for social justice, he pushed up against the front counter, slammed his trembling fists down and said:

"That's the most bigoted thing I've ever heard in my life!"

For a moment he thought that the night-clerk was about to say something, about to sit up and spew Rousseau-like confessions and in doing so be a part of a faith healing to rival the greatest miracles of the Bible. After a blustery, fevered bout of wheezing and coughing, the night-clerk would wrench forth a despicable, tar-black string of confessions and be forgiven. But the night-clerk slept through it.

"This one must sleep with The Just," he said, incredulously. "He must have some kind of immaculate conscience to sleep through The Reckoning."

He looked down at his scuffed and muddied army boots and thought of young soldiers dying senselessly on the battle field, in their black, leather jump boots.

"No," said Juan, turning to walk away. "He isn't good or evil. He's indifferent. He just doesn't give a fuck about *Brother Juan's* plight. O.k., Brother John. Sleep well then."

As if he could give the slip to the bad feelings in his heart, he ducked into the stairwell, but they were already waiting for him when he got there, crawling around on the bottom step like a bunch of hairy wolf spiders. With a defeatist nod, he acknowledged their presence, their omnipresence, and sat down quietly beside them to brood awhile, cursing the night-clerk in all of his whiteness, cursing his sky blue eyes, his spindly nose and icy, Jutes' blood. He was about to bad mouth the night-clerk's dear old, German grandmother, too, when suddenly he felt a light tug and a great unraveling inside of himself. A frayed fiber on the magnificent tapestry that was his soul had snagged and it was coming undone.

"*Oh*," he said, surprised by it, but ironically detached, as if it were happening to somebody else. Turning his gaze inward, he became a quiet, outside observer of himself.

"Do you see how easily *he* went rambling down *that* road," he noted. "And *he* imagined all along that it would be a dark and treacherous, lonely mountain path, when really it was a grand, well-lit, bustling avenue?"

He listened to the soft, electric hum of the mysterious light at the top of the stairwell, and added, "Ah, but it's not too late for *him* to turn back!"

To go back and start over again, to fashion, as it were, a means of reversing time, of undoing thought, emotion and memory, was what he wanted. It was the great trick, the last splendid gambit that he would now attempt. The only question was whether or not he could actually pull off such an ambitious hoax? Could he fool himself into believing that he could make the hatred mushrooming in his heart disappear for good? Why not. The world, after all, was made up of tricks. Tricks and very few miracles. It would require sleight of hand, a bit of self-talk. The subconscious mind, if you harped on it long enough, eventually believed exactly what it was told. But at the moment, the only thing that he could muster were distractions, thin smoke and cracked mirrors. A trifling lot came to mind.

It was cold on the landing and it smelled of damp concrete, didn't it? Yes, like the Los Angeles riverbed, like the graffitied mouths of sewer tunnels that were his playgrounds as a boy. He spat over the stair railing, a rainbow arch vanishing into the darkness below, without a sound. There was something about the silence in the stairwell that made him think of the dramatic hush in the air after a symphony ends. Then the quiet turned on itself and he thought of loud noises, of heavy things falling and crashing to the earth from great heights, of bombs going off on quiet, Midwestern suburban streets. Terrible silence.

"He's got some balls," he finally said, turning to walk down that road again. "To sit there and tell me, *'Speq, bij ruz speq.'* Who the fuck does he think he is?"

He wanted to strangle the night-clerk in his sleep and burn Chadwick Hall to the ground. He wanted the world to see an inferno atop Spangler Hill, a pyre lighting up the misty predawn, and to feel the guiltless bliss of knowing that the night-clerk's smoldering bones were buried beneath the charred roof and rafters and still-smoking embers. Every part of him wanted it— his adrenal glands pumped epinephrine like hot, crude oil into his bloodstream, a fiery and bilious sea rose up in his gallbladder and his head throbbed and wailed:

Kill the son of a bitch, set fire to the whole fucking thing and run! Into the trees!

Any jury, of his peers or of his superiors, and any judge, for or against the death penalty, would acquit him outright on a plea of insanity, because they'd see, as he did at the moment, that there were exceptions to the law against murdering one's fellow man. It was perfectly okay to kill a man if he treated you like a dog, wasn't it? It was a minor bylaw anyhow. Why else was it so far down on the list of that obscure Decalogue? But then again, he thought, maybe the night-clerk was innocent and someone else was to blame. Now that the idea occurred to him, there really was no great mystery. He needn't look any further than the first law on the list for hard proof. It mentioned the author and perpetrator by name, the Maker of the laws and the Perp, as one in the same. Yes, and the next three or four commandments seemingly offered even more damning evidence of this, confirming, at least in Juan's mind, exactly with whom the fault lay for his miserable life. Altogether they painted an unflattering image of an egocentric, wrathful and petty, if omnipotent, Being, whose love was conditional and who, in all of His supposed wisdom, was still bias, which is to say that He had His favorites and least favorites among men. And in this light Juan was neither. He was a dog. He looked wistfully to the top of the stairwell. He was up there somewhere, beyond the endless spiral of iron railing, the random swatches of light, and the hundred sixty-one steps. He was up there and would now have to answer for the poorly designed existence of one man in particular. Juan was talking back to God, thinking, *why've you created me so? The Potter has no rights over the lump of clay,* as he went flying up the stairs, wrapped in God's own anger. He was now at war with Him.

Ascending on raven's wings, he rose up into the strange, new lunar heights of the sixth, seventh, and eighth stories of the stairwell. He'd never gone up so high before. He was pretty much a lower level dweller, because he didn't know anybody up there, and nobody up there knew him. However, on occasion Juan did listen in on their conversations. The stairwell is where they'd go to have serious talks of a personal nature, and he had gleaned sordid bits and pieces of their secret lives as their discrete murmurs drifted down to the bottom, where he sat from time to time after nightfall. They talked about what college kids sometimes talk about—the insufferable tragedies of youth, the hardships of homesickness,

182

the horror of abusive boyfriends, date rape and abortion, affliction, too, eating disorders, depression, alcoholism, drug addiction, and seemingly innocent gossip about gay roommates. If they were suffering, Juan had prayed for them. If they were the cause of suffering, he had prayed for them, too. He had considered how all human beings suffer, but how not all suffering was the same. The disquietude in his own soul was because of who he was or rather because of who he was *not*. He thought about this now, as he rose above the ninth, tenth and eleventh floors, as he overcame the cold and the darkness and the solitude of the stairwell and of the world.

There was a landing at the top, and a single 60-watt light flickering above a narrow, steel-plated door. He looked around, somewhat disappointed, and shrugged. If this is all there was, then he didn't see why people made such a fuss. But if He was everywhere, as they say, He was here, too, in this small, poorly lit, insignificant space.

"Funny," Juan said snidely. "I honestly thought that You'd be much bigger."

He wanted some kind of reaction to this remark—boils on his testicles, lightening up his ass—something to let him know that He was listening and was displeased. But He didn't answer, didn't hear him or wasn't inclined to justify Himself to the likes of him. And already he sensed the moment slipping away, the anger and the object of his anger slipping away, out through the corroded keyhole in the steel-plated door, out onto the rooftop. But Juan wasn't going to let it go, because he was not, despite prevailing opinions, a mechanical, mail-order monkey who would eventually wind down. He was a man who had come to do this one thing,

183

moving of his own volition, on his own two feet, with nothing now to stop him—not the door, not the old, cast iron, pin-tumbler padlock securing the door, and least of all not Him on the other side of the door. Juan was going to do whatever he damn well wanted to do and what he wanted was to storm the rooftop of Chadwick Hall and face Him like a man.

The door was an afterthought. He didn't even see it. He looked right through it, at the nightscape of stars frittering away and the waning spring moon, and the door quickly gave way. Without so much as a wriggle on the doorknob, all of the things that constituted the door came crashing down at his feet—rusty rivets popped and clinked on the landing, the heavy, steel plating buckled, broke apart and fell in twisted shards, the hinges turned to dust and the planks and battens cracked and splintered. All hot with rage and hardened by resolve, his face was suddenly cooled by a night breeze as he stared silently through the open rectangle of darkness, the doorway to the roof. He would've liked to say that he dreamt that it would happen this way, this moment, exactly as it was happening. But if he had dreamt it as such it would definitely have turned out differently. Charging blindly through the open doorway, over the freshly fallen rubble that once was the door, he stepped onto the roof, not knowing what was waiting for him out there. And the feeling of not knowing was exhilarating!

"If You're really against me," he said, picking up right where he'd left off, "then who the fuck can be for me?"

It wasn't meant to be rhetorical, but neither was he expecting Him to answer. Stumbling blindly across the gravelly rooftop, as if crossing a darkling plain, he lost his footing at every step, but somehow managed to keep the answer to himself, all roiled up in his heart with equal parts indignation, self-importance and pride. Finally, he slipped and dropped to his knees, but quickly sprang to his feet and let it fly, howling:

"Who can be for me, but *me?*"

And the way he said it was as if he were flipping God the bird. It went on like this for who knows how long, him raving in the seditious tongues of fallen angels, like all of those bearded, bleary-eyed, yobbish heretics who had gone before him, perched up on snowy mountaintops, striking savagely at the night sky, saying all of the things that Job would not say. But after all of this, nothing happened. Juan didn't sink into the icy, turbulent, black water straits of a personal purgatory for all of the things he'd said and done. It seems He was merciful after all, and had a sense of humor, too, because He hadn't cursed him in His heart. His *heart*—that thing that men call the divine heart—was burning for him, hotter and brighter than any Christian hell, blazing like a mighty, eternal, benevolent flame. Naturally, Juan had no earthly way of knowing this, and even if he did, he would be incapable of conceptualizing it, because past experience precluded it. Then again, it was probably best that he didn't know the truth about how He really felt. It would have left him wondering why He hadn't just come out and said so to begin with. Truthfully, Juan would've shaken his fist and insisted, *Faith, like salvation, must be earned.*

He went on ranting, pointing the accusing finger skyward, failing to see, in his present state of mind, where the roof ended and the night sky, dying in the periwinkle light of the coming day, began.

"You've got a job to do," he said, his toes hanging over the edge of the roof. "You can't just sit around like some big, dumb

Greek god on the mount and play favorites! You can't just sit back and let shit happen! You've got to save me, too, because I'm your son. Well?"

After standing there for a hundred winters, nothing happened. Nothing, he realized, would ever happen, at least not while he was still alive. So he set out to make *something* happen. As casual as a man on a Sunday morning stroll, who steps lightly off of a curb, he put one foot forward and stepped off of the roof. He made a show of it, too, without meaning to, plummeting headfirst, back arched slightly, arms stretched out to the sides, a perfect swan dive, irrespective of the concrete below. Facing the windows of Chadwick Hall as he fell, he sort of smiled, an ironic grin, thinking how peculiar the world looked upside down.

The view flashed by in quick succession—a darkened windowpane, a darkened windowpane, a Chinese exchange student reading in bed by lamplight, a darkened windowpane, a darkened windowpane, a darkened windowpane, a sexy, white co-ed smoking a cigarette at her window, gasping low as Juan whizzed by, and of course his own reflection in every darkened windowpane. He decided that his own death, in this fashion, was his revenge on America and God or whomever for having lived a short life of inequity. He hadn't left a suicide note to explain it all, but figured that somehow people would simply understand. But before he hit the pavement, a strong, auspicious wind lifted up his body, landing him back on the roof, squarely on his ass.

What were you praying for all of this time, it asked, *in your heart?*

Remorseful, he looked up at the sky and said: "Pardon me Sir, I meant not to do it."

14

Juan hadn't spoken a word to anyone about that night on the roof. Who was he going to tell anyway? There were no clerics sitting in ornate confessionals, waiting in the faint, solemn light of the mahogany box to hear what he had to say, because as he whispered his sins through the lattice the old priest, with the feathery white cap of hair, would clutch at his chest, struggle for breath and wheeze: "S-sin-sinner!" There were no college mental health counselors sitting in the clinical university offices of Kaplan Hall, the psychology building, who could help him, because the minute they heard his story they'd report it to the proper authorities as a case of attempted suicide and promptly have him committed to a psych hospital. There were actually diseased rats in the basement of Chadwick Hall whom he trusted more. He talked to the rats. He swore them all to secrecy and told them that for him the incident on the roof was something like being struck by lightning. It was a freakishly rare occurrence which, if you survived it, changed your fate, turning a hard life into a miracle existence. He told the rats that he actually wanted to die that night and wondered if having been saved from a personal extinction was not, if fact, a life sentence. What he didn't say, what he'd kept stowed in his impenitent heart was this:

Priests, therapists and rats. Intermediaries all. God knows what I've done.

This is not to say that he felt he had to make things right with God. He might have added, with the indignant pluck of a feral tomcat pulled wet and writhing from a certain river death, that God had yet to make things right with him, alleging:

"God knows what He's done to me and what He has to do to make it right."

Of course, Juan wouldn't dream of asking for that one special privilege which no one spoke of, the one advantage conferred upon his white classmates at birth, an inherent advantage, as blatant as the first-move advantage in chess, a privilege which lived on through ignorance and silent collusion. All he wanted was his sanity at the end of the day and a baccalaureate degree at the end of the semester. It might have been too much to ask for, but he couldn't possibly settle for anything less.

"I'll do what I can," he said, sitting down to study in his dorm. "So, God shall oblige."

It was the week of finals and upstairs they were cramming for exams, everyone half-heartedly occupied in the undergraduate's long practiced and paradoxically undisciplined art of stuffing weeks' worth of syllabus readings into a single night; whatever would fit into the undersized compartment of short-term memory. It meant sleep deprivation and dwindling mental capacity, until the students were more vegetable than human, but it didn't seem to discourage them from counting down, with surprising exuberance, the very minutes to the Midnight Yell. This was the university tradition where students screamed from the open windows, balconies and rooftops of their dorms, apartments and rented houses at the stroke of midnight to release pre-finals stress. Through the late hours of the evening, over aperitifs and hot suppers, they plotted in brilliant detail exactly what it was they planned to do in the span of those twelve magical chimes, in that cathartic time of sanctioned madness. There would be obscenities shouted at egg-headed professors and their lackey teaching assistants, too, Wagner operas blaring from the top floor, Tarzan yelps, sex noises, buglers blowing reveille, bottle rockets shot whistling into the sycamore trees on the winding Ashford Road and ten thousand other students howling like the ghosts of all those who had died too young. Lording beamishly over all of those crazy kids, over the whole, chaotic affair, would be the full, august moon.

He looked up sleepily and sort of sideways from *Beowulf* on his lap, looked to the ever-widening cracks in the plaster on the southern wall of his dorm-room. If he could see through walls, he'd be looking directly at the great, green oxidized face of the bronze clock, shining by incandescent floodlights atop Farrington's Obelisk, on the other side of campus. Unceremoniously, he'd note the hour, not the least bit interested in the time. The night was passing away, the clock ticking away its last breath, and he wished it a quick death. He wished that the fanciful, baroque hands, each one as tall as a man, would spin like propellers and fly passed the midnight hour, because he didn't care for the Midnight Yell at all. It was a strange tradition, really.

The first time Juan heard the screams, he thought it was the end of the world. That night, freshman year, he went to bed with William Shakespeare, all of his collected works, histories, comedies, dramas and tragedies, and was awakened by a young woman's tortured wailing. *Like this it ends*, he thought, *with all of the Western hemisphere in darkness and me in my underwear, and not yet a college graduate.* But her screams quickly evolved into a comical, somewhat juvenile, heart-felt harangue.

"Fuck finals, neighbors!" she shouted, laughing. "Fuck finals, Professor Drake!"

Then, as he got out of bed to see what was going on, the drunken fraternity brothers started in, yipping like a pack of wild coyotes from the neat, white rank of frat houses across the road. He shuffled barefoot to the transom window, fingered at the latch, turned it and pulled the chain. He hadn't opened it in months, and for good reason. A salvo of empty beer bottles rained down on the parking lot, shattering in a curiously wide range of pitches, like some dangerous, new musical instrument. A naked student, wearing nothing but white tennis shoes, came running across the lot, weaving in between parked cars, and stopped to catch his breath right outside of Juan's dorm-room window. He cast a long shadow on the translucent windowpane, which seemed to stretch as the student, in a deceptively light-hearted tone, shouted into the night:

"If I flunk I'm going to shoot the dean of admissions for letting me into this shitty school in the first place!"

That was freshman year. What he didn't know then was that all of this to-do was a local custom, just as if he were to travel to another place and time and were to witness an act so bizarre it defied logic. Any one of the midnight revelers, any high-spirited, young woman or man, of average intelligence and a sense of history, would have said as much, if cornered that night in a study lounge or in a stairwell going in between floors.

If asked why they had joined in on this riotous, late night romp they'd say that the Midnight Yell was the Chinese tradition of feet binding, the ancient practice of self-mummification and the ritual of Tibetan sky burial all balled up into one; all of the beautiful, sacred and mysterious parts, without the breaking of bones and deformity of limbs, without the drinking of poisonous, urushi tea and slow death, and without the mutilation of the dead and the lavish, mountaintop feast for the birds of prey. Still, it wouldn't have made this collegiate tradition any less strange or frightening for Juan, a quiet Mexican-American boy from the eastside, new to the school. Back home, where he grew up, if someone screamed like that the neighbors called the cops. But here at university, a person could scream at midnight and the campus police wouldn't bother to show up, because they figured it was just a bunch of spoiled, rich college kids shouting about how miserable they were, about how hard life was, because they had to take a few exams in the morning.

A senior now, Juan still would have felt slightly awkward, even a bit ridiculous, participating in the Midnight Yell. Not because it wasn't a sufficiently grand or an excessively sophomoric tradition. It had the distinct quality that appealed to those who took part for the sake of foolishness and to those who had an authentic interest in the whole experience, as would a cultural anthropologist. It was just that Juan didn't know what to yell when the time came, wasn't quite sure what words fit the occasion.

He once saw everything worth saying and not worth saying on the walls of a bowling alley bathroom stall, all of the low, vulgar, despicable, bigoted things ever said and all of the witty, poetic, philosophical, spiritual things, too. It was all there for him to choose from, preserved in a crystalline memory of that stall. And yet, he wasn't even sure that anyone would hear him way down there, bellowing from his poorly-lit, hole of a dorm-room, out to the empty parking lot. To spite the revelers, he kept quiet, sat like the nervous wonk that he was, re-reading *Beowulf*, occasionally indulging in mental distractions.

"When we last left off," he said, flipping through the pages, "our hero Grendel, the Terribly Lonely Hall-Stalker, was going home, sick to his stomach after having spent all night ransacking famed and gabled halls, gobbling up pugnacious little nobles. Home was far away, it always is. Home was across bleak and boundless steppes and miles of misty peat bogs. It was on the other side of the ice-capped peaks at the top of the world, passed a weird looking lake whose steely black surface cast no reflections. Passed the blood stained, catacomb cliffs beside the northern sea, the beach below strewn with whale bones and the cracked and salted skulls of Scandinavian kings. Passed the horizon, which he'd cross at a trot, as if it were the finish line. There, electrical storm clouds had gathered, hanging low in the pale sky. There, upon a stretch of weathering shale, was a grove of moss-covered, god-like trees. And in a craggy hole in the ground, underneath those great, god-like trees, was his home. His mother, that dear, doting wretch of a woman, was waiting for him down there, sharpening the tips of her gnarled claws against the bedrock. Grendel, it seems, had nothing, but he had a mother. And although the light of the coming day didn't shine down in the depths of their cave, his mother would still be able to see him clearly in the darkness. Yes, he was going to hell for sure for what he'd done, but as for now he was going home."

Juan was happy for Grendel, genuinely happy for this his sort of homecoming. Sometimes an emotion like happiness filtered through sadness and so was felt very little. Other times, like now, it came all at once, like a thunderstorm after a long drought, and was felt intensely, to the point that he himself began to feel homesick. He wanted to go home, wanted to be in Boyle Heights again, wanted to see his mother and be comforted and tormented by the familiar. And for once in his life he did not try to analyze the feeling, did not over think it. There was no musing, no, *Home is the same place for everyone and so is the yearning for it.* There was none of this, *Homesickness is memory traces, passed on from the very first wanderer trying to find his way back home.* He simply sat back and invented fantastic homecoming scenarios in the whimsical part of his heart.

"You will go home like Grendel, the Dark Saint," he said, "a broken hearted berserker with fresh blood on your hands and absolutely no memory of the crime. And the school newspaper will tell a grisly story of murder on the campus of a major, California university on a warm, June night during the Midnight Yell. Oooo! Murder! Murder most foul!"

He turned the book over, making a little tent out of it on his lap.

"No, that won't do," he said, swatting at the dank, dormitory room air, at the thought itself, a pesky wasp trying to sting him.

The alternative was just as glum, but more romantic in his eyes.

"You will go home like *what's-his-name*, a dead hero in a sugar pine box, and your people will mourn you. They will wash your body, your young body with few physical scars, in the green waters, the cigarette-butted, aluminum-can glutted, green-algae waters of

Hollenbeck Lake. Then twelve big, bad ass *cholos*—the rightful Lords of White Bluffs and all of Boyle Heights proper, hard, street smart men who studied all of their lives to be who they are and earned doctorates in *Vatoism* from the finest correctional institutions in California: Folsom, Chino and Pelican Bay—will dress you in fine, traditional garb, a white T-shirt, a black and white flannel Pendleton, buttoned only at the top, khaki pants, creased just so, and shiny-black, spit-shined shoes. *¡Firme!* In tribute they'll tattoo *School Boy* on your right forearm and put a brand-new # 2 pencil in your shirt pocket. *¡Qué firme!* They will set to work on chopping down a half an acre of Hollenbeck mahoganies to build you a funeral pyre. Not just any old pyre either, like *what's-his-name's*, but a grand pyre, as big as a hill. Ten days it'll take to build the thing. Then they'll wrap you up tightly in a golden sarape made of wild goat's fur and the 2nd finest silk in the world, and lie you flat on the hill of logs, under an endless, silver sky."

"Oh, and don't forget the grave offerings! Twelve precious little gifts for the dearly departed: a pewter, dashboard Virgen de Guadalupe (her eyes crossed, her mouth kind of crooked), a rare, Mexican coin from the short reign of Emperor Maximilian (silver, eight Reales, the imaginary bust of the executed king faded now) a crinkled, black and white postcard of a 1948 Chevy Bomb with a dedication: *Lalo's Last Ride,* six perfectly round, marble-sized obsidian stones, relics of Tenochtitlan (or maybe they're just cheap black marbles, who the hell would give a dead man marbles?), a medium-sized pen knife with the initials C.K. etched into the handle, a brass key that unlocks a door somewhere, what else? A half a dozen other things, sentimental things, special things. As they tuck the personal offerings in between your feet and around

194

your head and hands, the twelve, big, bad ass *cholos* will break down crying, sobbing uncontrollably:

He's dead, School Boy is dead!

"They will douse your funeral pyre in gasoline and light it on fire. And it will burn for days and days, because the Boyle Heights Fire Department won't come to put it out. It'd do no good to try and put it out. It'd take a thousand fire brigades to battle it, shooting water cannons at it from all sides, attacking it by air, too, with a fleet of water bombers. The hoses would run dry and go limp in their hands. The air-tankers would run out of petrol and crash land. So maybe they'll resort to flying fire-copters over Sherman Oaks, Van Nuys, Tarzana, Westwood, Beverly Hills, and Pacific Palisades, looking for swimming pools into which they'll dip their big water-buckets. They'll drain every last pool and still won't be able to contain the blaze. So, they'll sit down on the steps of their fire engines, coughing up smoke, looking perplexed, their faces all sweaty and blackened by soot. In the end they'll throw their hands up and pray for rain. No, it'd do no good to try and put out the fire. God Himself couldn't put it out if He wanted to. Anyway, they'll know that it's not some abandoned warehouse fire, just by the smell in the air, because nothing else smells like the stench of human flesh burning—a sweet, pungent, nauseating scent. They'll know that it's *your* funeral pyre burning and they will let it burn. People will see the smoke and flames from as far away as the Pacific Coast Highway."

He must have been well loved, they'll say. *God's own favorite.*

"It's what they'll say, anyway, what they'll infer by the looks of the inferno burning in the east. The church elders will see the smoke, too, sitting solemnly on their pews at eight o'clock Mass.

Turning slowly from the alter, they'll see the thick, shadowy pillar rising up to heaven, see it blotting out the colors of the stain-glass windows of good Saint Mary's Parish, blotting out the sun itself. Wait until the Mass has ended, until the priest dismisses them, then they'll come hobbling out one by one, with Catholic prayers for every occasion. Accustomed, at their age, to attending funerals regularly, they'll stand around, veiled and hats in hand, sucking at their toothless gums, paying their last respects, mumbling, *Whose funeral is that anyway? Doña who? Didn't she die last winter? Oh, the Bitol boy? Oh, him. Okay.* Ultimately indifferent to this poor boy's death, they'll say nothing more. They'll just stand around, stoic-faced, sucking at their gums. God meant it to be so."

"The neighborhood kids will come running from their empty lots and playgrounds, to watch the glorious bonfire and the mysterious red smoke in silent wonder. They won't have the words to say what they're feeling, but they'll be thinking:

They didn't put him in the ground 'cause it would take him too long to dig his way out and get to heaven. They put him right into the fire and he went straight to God.

"Children know that much about death. Even though the coroner's report will note the official cause of death was accidental, the children will know what really happened. They'll stand there watching the coils of smoke spiraling skyward, your withered soul all tangled up in it, the overcast sky breathing it in, God inhaling, His lungs getting full."

Bye bye, they'll say, waving their chubby little hands. *Go to God.*

"Children know more about death than you and I."

"Then, over the crackle and roar of flames, over the sputter of smoldering bones and the thunder of burning timber, will come a wave of inconsolable wailing. It is the woman who went mad with sorrow. See her squatting there, by the blazing funeral pyre, her loose gray hair blowing wildly in the wind? See her screaming and clawing at her once beautiful face, yanking out her teeth and trying to throw herself into the fire to ease her own suffering?"

That's the mother, they'll whisper to one another. *Poor old woman.*

"Woe! What a sad day! Woe! What a tragedy, the death of young Juan Juárez Bitol."

He stared wistfully at the transom window and suddenly laughed out loud.

"No, that crap won't do," he said, swatting furiously at the air.

Another scenario was rounding the corner of his mind. He saw his own future clearly, saw a joyful homecoming. It was as if sadness and happiness were two pages in the same book, but somehow they'd gotten stuck together, so he never got the chance to read the part about happiness. But now the pages had come unstuck, if only for a brief moment, and he saw the hidden page peeking out from underneath. And as he peeled it back there it was, a happy ending.

"Yes," he said, tossing *Beowulf* onto the floor. "That's how it'll be."

He let the idyllic new vision of homecoming flower in his head, smiling as it unveiled itself, marveling at the sight of it, his eyes sparkling like those of a child's eyes reflecting skyrockets exploding in the night sky. What a show! He wanted to get excited and shout about it out the transom window, and in doing so beat the others to the Midnight Yell festivities by a few hours, but all that he could muster was a smile.

Quietly then, very quietly, he bent down, picked up the second-hand copy of the *Norton Anthology of English Literature* lying on the floor, turned to the dog-eared page of *Beowulf* and continued reading.

It was late, but not quite midnight. He opened his eyes, dabbed fresh, hot drool from his lips, and had the strangest feeling that he'd slept through the Midnight Yell. Something in the uncertain light of the flickering banker's lamp made him certain of it. Earlier that night, he'd scribbled marginal notes to himself in *Beowulf* as cues of what to listen for in the hours leading up to midnight. And like signs of an apocalypse, Juan read them one by one:

"Listen carefully for people talking non-stop, for talking addicts who won't shut the fuck up, on-and-on-anon*ymous*; listen closely for any mention of midnight, insanity or death of any sort. Listen for the sound of forelaughter, which is laughter in advance of a good time, in anticipation of good times to come; listen for the sound of Farrington's bells tolling and for the sound of drums."

But it was so quiet and he wished he hadn't written any of it, especially the part about people talking incessantly, because the emptiness of it, of the silence, worried him.

"Is anybody there," he asked.

The silence did not answer, so he appealed to it, asked, "Won't somebody say something?"

Nobody said anything and he started to panic. He scooted across the mattress, put an ear against the wall and listened for

198

signs of life. At first there were watery sounds, a ghostly gurgle and rush inside hundred-year old pipes, flowing downwards and upwards, obeying and defying gravity in quick turns. Wasn't water a good sign, an indication that life could, in fact, exist? Like the detection of water on Mars signaled habitable conditions. And so also inside the walls of Chadwick Hall? He listened closely, patiently, and the great wall suddenly became what he wanted it to be, a gigantic switchboard connecting him to the upstairs residents. He could hear everything now, *everything*— the turning of a textbook page, sighs, snores, a sneeze, footfall, human voices, inflections and all. And the lives of others never sounded so comforting.

Up in a second story dorm-room, a coed was warming up her vocal cords for the Midnight Yell, lubricating them not with scales, but with laughter and wine. She sounded quite drunk and very attractive and, although Juan was undersexed by nature, he wondered what she looked like and even began fantasizing about her.

A petite, green-eyed brunette by the name of Anne, he thought, *Anne Aynesworth of Orange County, with a shingle bob hairdo, a dark, surfer-girl figure and a quirky grin.*

But he quickly went as limp as a flat tire when he heard a second voice, that of the charming, young male student sitting next to her in her dorm-room. He was telling her really bad jokes, trying to get her into bed and she, like a dumb fish, laughed, took the bait.

In another dorm-room, a demented music major, most likely high on acid, was playing an antique Theremin. The eerie, high tremolo noises vibrated in his eardrum, a robotic, non-human sound that made him think of a 1950s black-and-white sci-fi film wherein a race of giant robots invade earth and kill all but *one* of its inhabitants. What whimsy!

A toilet was flushed repeatedly in a seventh floor lavatory and again came a surge of water through the rusty pipes, flowing by starts and fits, clogging at the joints, thick with wads of toilet tissue and human excrement. If this wasn't a sign of life, he didn't know what was. When it finally rolled sluggishly passed the section of sewage-line where he'd been listening, the pipe cracked and something seeped out. Philosophical crap, a piffled rendering of the priority of definitional knowledge:

"If Q fails to know what J-ness is, then Q fails to know anything about J-ness."

He didn't pretend to understand what it meant, but had enough common sense to know that somebody up there was talking about him, telling lies about him, working him into the equation, as it were, and he had a suspicion that he was about to be up to his nose in it. Inside of the wall, the pipe continued to come apart, the crack slowly spreading under the constant strain of the tons of sewage coming down.

"It won't hold . . ." he grunted, ". . . very much longer . . . any second now . . ."

The line ruptured, a sound like Chadwick Hall itself having a tremendous bowel movement and now it all came oozing out—a foul, garbled deluged of human filth, filling up the empty spaces in between the wall, filling up the silence. He didn't want to give it credence by paying attention to it, but reasoned that it was the only way to determine whether or not he had real cause for alarm.

In defense of J, he pressed his ear closer to the wall and listened.

I've heard dorm dwellers, residential counselors and my beloved fraternity brothers who live in the row across the way tell strange stories, saying that they themselves have seen a thing in the shape of a man roaming Spangler Hill after dark, squatting under the Torrey pines, gnawing on succulent feeder roots, sniffing raccoon shit, wondering what is it is it to eat, sticking darkling beetles up his asshole and, after everyone has turned down the lights and gone to bed, gliding across the parking lot under a veil of black clouds and crawling into Chadwick Hall through an open transom. Dorm dwellers in the old days called him Wodewose. Wodewose the wild man. Wodewose the godless primitive who doesn't know what he is or why he's here and definitely doesn't fit into this world. And yet here's this big, swarthy, hairy, smeared-around-the-back orangutan, living in the basement of our hall. They say that he's been down there for a hundred years, living underground with the grubs and the spiders and the snakes and the moles and the petrified bones of dead things, long before the hall was even built. But if it's only been a day it's still one day too long. And maybe he's not alone! What if there's a hundred others just like him rooting around down there in the dark—newborns, juveniles, mature adult males and females, destroying university property, smearing their feces on the walls, yanking high voltage wires straight out of the electrical panel and swinging from the overhead pipes until they burst and water floods the basement? But if he's the only one it's still one too many. It's been said that they have the ability to reproduce at an alarming rate, because they're asexual, hermaphrodites or some such thing. They don't fuck, they just spawn, like fungi or snails. Clearly a danger to those of us from the best of houses. God help us! God strike him dead!

He waited for the deathblow to come, presumably in the form of an avenging, blue-eyed archangel with flowing blonde locks and a serene, and oddly feminine face. It would descend silently, its blood red, Roman cloak billowing every time it beat its sprawling, aquiline wings. And its sterling virtue and golden, breastplate armor would blind him, damned fool, so that he would not see the fiery, revolving sword coming down to smite him.

Yet when he considered the odds of it actually happening this way he had to laugh, realizing that it wasn't realistic at all.

"No, not like that," he said. "He wouldn't waste an archangel's precious time on me."

Lowering his head for a moment, he pictured it differently.

"And God's own boot will squash *him*," he said. "Like a dung beetle, and he will be scrapped off of His heel with a stick. Yes, that's it. What an exit!"

Try as one might, there was no easy way to escape one's fate. The book that he'd been reading all night long (it may as well have been his Bible for the faith he put in it) told him as much. When it was your time to go, it was your time, no matter if you retreated to a faraway country or hid beneath your bed. But this didn't keep him from making one final, passive-aggressive gesture of defiance against those who wanted him dead. Looking toward the ceiling, he began spouting a kind of apocalyptic, nonsense poem, drawn from memory, though parts of it he improvised. As he murmured each line, his lips twisted into involuntary smirks:

From the high plateau, where he could not go, a voice called out to him below: 'We're doomed,' it said, 'we're clearly doomed, for having so offended thee!'

And he, because he could not see, simply grinned and squealed with glee:

'Yes, it seems you're likely doomed, I cannot say for sure. But it

202

sounds like doom and it looks like doom, so yes, I'd say you're all quite doomed!'

He got some satisfaction out of this, but the feeling was fleeting and left only an anemic little grin on his face, which slowly waned as he put his ear to the great and all-knowing wall again to listen for the endgame. They were still yammering away up there, in theory-speak, in the self-important, egg headed jargon of college students.

In point of fact, God will not strike him dead. It is not God's work. It is Man's work. God cannot do what we must do for ourselves. That being said, we have, as I see it, two postulates before us, id est, one of two feasible options.

"Yes," said Juan, nodding attentively. "Go on."

The first is death, id est, we kill him, quickly and inconspicuously, a quiet midnight lynching, for example, and make it look like just another dorm-room suicide.

"Uh-huh, I've heard that one before," said Juan. "Very unoriginal. What else?"

The second is castration, id est, we cut off his hairy balls to stop him from breeding.

His testicles yoyo-ed into his stomach and dangled there tautly, as visions of portly eunuchs mounted on fat geldings galloped around in his head. They all sang treble through their tears and whispered to their horses:

"Listen. You'll want to pay special attention to this next part, to what they're about to say." *Castration. Aye! Aye! Aye! The ayes have it! Castration!*

It was the last thing that he heard before silence, before terrible silence, which meant that they were already on their way down to the basement.

"If they take the stairs," he said, "they'll be here in two minutes, tops."

He stared at the door, nodding, saying, "Okay then, come on," then laid down, submissive as a lamb, waiting for them to kick it down, while objectively wondering:

What will they do with my pretty testicles? Put them on exhibit in a big glass jar of formaldehyde, like Joaquin Murrieta's hansom, decapitated head, and sell tickets to the student body to see them? 'Come one come all, see the veritable hairy balls of the thing that lives in the basement of Chadwick Hall! That's right ladies and gentlemen, the thing's hairy balls! Is it an animal, is it human, is it an extraordinary freak of nature, or is it the long sought after link between Man and Orangutan, which naturalists have decided does exist, but which has hitherto been undiscovered? Come one come all! See the thing's hairy balls!' Will they eat my plump testicles, like some rare delicacy, like bulls' testes prepared à la Nage or better yet à la Nads, served to foreign dignitaries after the bullfight? Ah, but more importantly, what will I do without my testicles?

Juan stuck his hand down his pants and fondled his testicles, as if they were a pair of newborn, baby sparrows in their nest. He really didn't have a clue as to why grown men did this, whether it was an act of juvenile bravado, saying to the world, *Look, I got balls! I can make many babies!* or if they were actually just making sure that they still had them way down there in their trousers. For his own part, he was saying goodbye to the one hundred million sperm who would not reach the egg, to the witnesses of his virility and to the dream of the wandering Mexican who came to this country to become a nation, great, strong and numerous. It was all that he could do, because he was tied up, as if with strong ropes, by the aphorism in *Beowulf*, which claimed:

204

There is no easy way to flee from one's Fate- try as one may!

All along, as he lay doubting the possibility of changing the course of things, *something* was calling out to him, as silent as subterranean water flowing through silt, a subconscious river trying to find daylight and a sea of consciousness. The tenor of it was hard, like that of a disappointed father pointing out a son's shortcomings for the sake of provoking a reaction.

Pinche pendejo, it chided, *you're not actually going to lie there and let them take your huevos are you? Why don't you grow a pair and do something about it? What did Beowulf say? Fate often saves an undoomed man when his courage is good! ¿Qué no?*

And then it occurred to him, the thing that was about to happen to him, and suddenly horrified by this particular, fatalistic string of logic, he broke free, ranting:

"Oh shit! They want to cut off my balls! Hold on now! Hold on! Wait a minute now! Wait a *pinche* minute! That can't happen! I can't let that happen! Up and out!"

He found himself saying these words over and over as he rolled out of bed and got to his feet, disoriented by the flickering, strobe light effect of the defective banker's lamp.

"By the time they get here I'll be gone," he said, stumbling barefoot to the writing table by the transom window. This was the extent of his escape plan and was a triumph in itself for a young man who had spent a lifetime thinking things through to the nth degree, until thought killed all possibility of action. Now it was apparent to him that to stop and think it over meant death, for him and for the entire, unborn generation in his scrotum. One supple gesture, one genocidal snip of the scissors and that would be the end of that.

The door was not a reliable exit, since the mob of castrators was presumably standing on the other side of it by now, readying themselves to knock it down. He looked instead to the transom window, irrespective of all the inherent flaws in its design, which made it nearly impossible to use as an escape route. First of all, there was its height from the floor and the risk of a fall and permanent paralysis. Then there was the danger of broken glass, as he would invariably try to squeeze his rather large head through the narrow opening, turning a potentially comic scene into an accidental beheading. It fared well for him that he wasn't thinking about this at all. There was only the impulse to rise from the dead the hundred million sperm in his scrotum, to keep the bloodline alive, an unseen hand moving him, pushing him, lifting him onto the little writing table by his shirt collar, urging him, *Up and out! Go now! Up and out!*

Atop of the table, he drew eye-level with the parking lot and through the open transom window saw glinting stars above the Torrey pines, prompting him to pause and detach in that moment of desperation and flight and exclaim:

"What a beautiful night!"

On an evening like this, he might have stared at the sky until dawn, until the sparrows finally twittered 'good day!' But looking over his shoulder, he could see the doorknob turning and the door itself bowing inward under the tremendous weight of an unseen rabble of devils.

Grendel must flee, he thought, *mortally sick, and seek his joyless home in the fen-slopes.*

Looking out of the transom window he said: "Time to go. And don't think I'll tell a soul about what happened down here, in this stinking hell. It's my secret. Up and out, balls and all!"

Someone must have fired a flare pistol into the night sky just then, because it was as if the sun burst through the darkness. All of Chadwick Hall saw it, too, and stopped whatever it was that they were doing to gawk at the inexplicable, atmospheric light spreading slowly across the nighttime sky, setting aglow solitary gray clouds and the rolling, mossy, wooded hills of this westside college town; illuminating, like electric-fire, cars in motion on poorly lit streets, every single building in the vicinity, the dumbfounded faces of onlookers walking their dogs, and the very curvature of the earth.

"Distractions," he muttered, "infinite distractions, without which everything would be the same, except without distractions."

As they were all transfixed on this phenomenon, no one actually witnessed his mysterious ascension from the basement. Nobody saw Juan rising barefoot through the transom window like a wisp of smoke, in the full form of a man, and finally alight on the hood of a BMW in the parking lot. He himself couldn't explain what had just happened, how he had ended up out there among the rows of parked cars, with his testes intact and the future of his yet-to-be born progeny secure. But he was glad for it, even as the divine subterfuge in the sky began to fade. The castrators had already barged into his dorm-room and, against his better judgment, he sat and watched them for a while from the relative safety of the lot. He couldn't see their faces, only saw their monstrous, white heads in silhouette, tottering around in the basement asylum that up until a minute ago he'd called home. They turned over and gutted his mattress, ransacked his closet, went through his personal belongings, his papers and all the books he'd read while at university, shouting Old English obscenities when they realized that he had somehow gotten away.

"It isn't over yet," he said. "I know their kind too well. They're an obstinate breed. It's how they managed to conquer the world. Come on. Don't stop. Keep going."

Like some hideous, man-sized hood ornament come to life, he hopped off of the BMW and started to make his way down Spangler Hill.

15

By the time he got to the bottom of Spangler Hill the night had already taken back the sky. It had swallowed every last particle of the miraculous light and had started in on the stars, decimating constellation after constellation until there was nothing left in the Northern Hemisphere and the heavens were unrecognizable.

"The modern sailor doesn't navigate by starlight anyhow," he said, trying hard to allay the fear. "He travels by electric light."

He was gazing ahead, at the occasional, accidental lamppost here and there along the brick path that meandered a quarter of a mile to the heart of campus. At first glance, their apparent magnitude seemed feeble, but as he got closer he saw a bright, imaginary line connecting them, saw that altogether they formed an arrow, not like Sagittarius' in the sky, but rather like the neon kind in a dark movie theater, marking the exit. It was showing him the way out and he followed it with blind abandon. He paid little attention to the screeching tires of the box truck that swerved into the opposite lane to avoid hitting him as he crossed University Drive. Oblivious, too, to the driver's death threats.

Pushing on, passed the intramural sports field, he thought that he heard the fraternity brothers out there in the dark, beyond the iron fence, playing a late night game of football.

"A game?" he said. "At this hour? In this poor light?"

Stopping for a moment he listened, put his ear to the night, as if it were a door.

It must have been the animalism of the sport that made their snap counts sound more like beastly snorts than human signals. Whatever the case, it frightened him and he had to scramble for mental distraction to steady his nerves.

"Well," he said, decidedly. "If it's a ritual I suppose it must be kept."

He had only spoken the words when it occurred to him that what he was hearing wasn't a bunch of blue-blooded, American college boys tossing a football around. The neat, herringbone-patterned path quivered lightly under his bare feet, every loosened brick a portent of the *thing* left unresolved, and a sign of those who were coming to lay it all to rest. Winged Hussars, he surmised, by the sound of things, by the pounding of horse-hooves on sod and the ominous whistle of flying, steel-clad horsemen charging across the intramural sports field. The horsemen of his very own, personal apocalypse, he presumed. The darkness was a veil and from it emerged six white men on black steeds; *La Migra*, the very same border patrolmen who had hunted his poor father in the wilds of Texas in 1959.

"In the name of ignorance and hate, they come," he said, describing what he saw. "Bent on genocide, they come. Wielding carbines, sabers and canisters of poisonous gas, they come. To shoot and hack off my manhood, they come. To poison my seed, they come. Like it or not, they come."

His retreat was a backwards march at a hundred paces a minute, to the still image of war horses at full trot, their bridles hot and slick with froth. And terrifying though it was, he wouldn't turn to run, because the act would violate his own personal code of manhood, which he had just now invented, and cheapen it so that his precious testicles, ironically, wouldn't be worth saving. So he walked in reverse, faced his fast approaching enemies and didn't turn until he reached the apparent sanctuary of the main square.

University Square, like Petrograd Square or the Zócalo in Mexico City, was a crossroads through which everything and everyone passed. Through it, at any given moment in the day, passed ten thousand students or more, their heads full of ideas yet to be conceptualized and dreams in utero, their young bodies rushing them off to lectures and seminars or trying to make it to their professors' office hours on time or up to Perkins Library for a study session or to the Student Union to cheer on the home team at the pep rally, and back again to dormitory halls at dusk. At this hour, however, there wasn't anybody around, except of course for the bronze statue of the university founder, old Doctor Woolsey in his fine, three-pieced tailored suit and pricey, wing-tipped Oxfords, his upturned eyes still watching the heavens.

"You again," said Juan, slowing to address him. "How come you look away whenever I walk by? I see the way you look so lovingly at the pretty blond girls who stroll by, and the white boy grad students always get a friendly wink or an encouraging, fatherly nod. What about me? Can't stand to see me wandering around your private campus? Can't stand to see what's become of your beloved university? You are a man of vision, the architect of this vast, academic empire, but you didn't see this coming: Mexicans matriculating en masse! The barbarians are inside the gates. So now what?"

As he stood there talking to the statue, a young white couple walked passed, strolling hand in hand towards midnight. The girl, suddenly catching a glimpse of Juan, was unable to mask her bewilderment at the sight of this dark, shaved headed, bare-footed mad man who, judging by the looks of it, was harassing old Doctor Woolsey's effigy.

"He doesn't have on any shoes," she whispered.

Embarrassed and panic-stricken in turn, the young man shooshed her, uncertain if Juan had overheard the remark.

God damn it Meagan, he wanted to say, *why can't you see he's not right in the head?*

But seeing Juan's crazed expression and fearing for their safety, the young man said nothing. They walked on, at a quicker pace, arm in arm now, and they did not look back.

"Well," said Juan, slapping a hand down on the plinth. "Nothing to say?"

Out of an unrequited sense of fairness, he waited for the good doctor to reply. The hands of the ancient clock atop Farrington's Obelisk cranked closer to midnight, the horsemen were bearing down, and still he waited for an answer.

"Pfff!" Woolsey finally said, turning up his nose.

A civilized show of contempt, befitting a man of letters. But Juan had a feeling that if the statue had a penis it would have pulled it out of its bronze trousers and urinated all over him. Why not. He would have done the same to the statue if he only had the time.

Memory told him to go straight to Perkins Library and to take the flight of stairs to the top floor, because it remembered the remarkable, sprawling view from up there, looking westward on a clear day, and the feeling of freedom it gave him to see the occasional wayward seagull wheeling over campus, returning on favorable winds to the Pacific Ocean. He had a good feeling that if he could make it up there before the Midnight Yell, everything would be okay, that his timely arrival to the portico of Perkins Library would automatically trigger an invisible mechanism that would yank out a stopper somewhere in the universe and all of his persecutors—the savage mob of castrators at Chadwick Hall, the white horsemen of his own private apocalypse, Brother John (the budding young bigot in his many manifestations) and Doctor Woolsey, the old, self-aggrandizing racist—would all be sucked right out of existence.

"And so shall it be," he said, crossing his fingers for good measure.

The path rose to meet him, up the slope that led to the uppermost parts of campus, through a forest of Norwegian pines and straight into his lingering fear of rabid squirrels.

"Beware the scaly-tailed, flying Beechey," he said in a low voice, "and shun the complexed-toothed Irawaddy, the tufted Squinney, the giant, fire-footed Guayaquil, 'cause they eat nuts and they eat young chickens. Here they come! One-two! One-two!"

All the way up the slope, he kept searching the grass and the shrubs and the trees for signs of nimble movements and bushy tails. He wasn't thinking about anything else. He hardly even noticed the midnight sermonizer who was sort of floating back and forth like a specter along the tree line, shouting damnation to the world. This man was a member of the Good Earth Harvesters' Church, the same old, long-bearded, crackpot holy man that he had seen down in the Village, on the corner of Bishop and Lowe, telling the passersby:

The weather is always the same, in Hell!

He remembered thinking at the time:

A street theologian. There's got to be some truth to what he's saying.

But tonight he wasn't worried about hell, not the fabled hell of the Good Book, the one the midnight sermonizer spoke of in the romantically macabre vernacular of religious zealots. It went something like, 'O eternity! On fire for eternity! Fire in the eyes! Fire in the mouth! Fire in the bowels! Woe, listen now to the sinners who have burned for a thousand years, and yet not one second has passed on God's clock! O eternity!'

Ah, but what does that midnight sermonizer know about hell anyway, thought Juan. *If Jesus were alive today he wouldn't be put to death on the cross, he'd be driven mad by this perverse generation. Trust me, I know. Hell? What does he know about hell?*

Hell was an afterthought. It could never be as real or as frightening to Juan as a dray of rabid squirrels. He was thinking of the squirrels and only after he got to the clearing at the top of the slope did he breathe a little easier.

The clearing was the grand, Northern Quad, the original site of the university in 1922. Rectangular in design, its silky green, Saint Augustine lawns and meticulously patterned, oak-tree lined, Italian brick paths sprawled out a full sixteen acres. Set stately at each corner of the quad was one of the "Four Founding Fathers", the first campus buildings—Grofhurst Hall to the north, Sotton Hall to the south, Tillman Hall to the west, and Perkins Library to the east. It was an impressive landscape by any standards, 'worth the price of admission,' a university counselor had mused during a tour of the campus for incoming freshman. In the daytime it looked very much like he imagined the grounds of the Palace of Versailles to look like—acres of open-air, miles of geometric gardens, marbled, Hellenistic-inspired fountains, and a spectacular canal, a thousand feet long, laid out to reflect the sun when it set. But the night had a certain way of turning the Northern Quad from popular campus spot to secret sanctuary. The now thinly lit grounds were deserted and, apart from the sound of night janitors and your resident ghosts, the halls were silent. Perkins Library, by nature, was silent and, though open late for Finals Week, looked practically empty, at least from the distance. He stared at it from across the quad, as his father had likely stared in wonder at the midnight lights of Brownsville, USA from across the river. Tonight, Perkins Library was more than brick and mortar pieced together in an aesthetically intriguing, architectural design. It was a golden-hued, fairyland basilica, a fortress of light— foot-lights casting conical halos against the Romanesque façade, oversized, electrical lanterns swaying in the colonnaded portico, making a summer solstice day of the entry way, and roof-mounted floodlights shining down, illuminating the way in.

As he got closer he shut his eyes, like a horse that knows the way home. The light shone through his eyelids and, colored shades of orange-pinkish-purple by the bloodstream, had a kind of blurred, kaleidoscopic effect. He stumbled towards it, clumsy and blind, felt his feet leaving the ground. It was like the dream of flying, so lucid and real, and all the while well aware that it is a dream. But he wasn't dreaming. He was *flying*, like a wayward seagull returning to the sea.

When the sensation of flight ended, Juan opened his eyes and realized that he was standing in the foyer of the library. The Reading Room, with its checkerboard floors, intricate brickwork, large, leadlight windows and high, vaulted ceilings, was set alight by giant, aqua-green, hanging lanterns. Against the back wall, the microfilm machines were lined up in a row, all of them having been left on, quietly humming the news of the day and news of days past. Seeing nobody around, he walked passed and started up the main staircase leading to the 2nd floor rotunda.

On the midway landing, a series of colorful mosaics inlaid in a wall, depicting university education, caught his eye. There was one that showed a balding alchemist, in shirtsleeves and a white lab apron, busy mixing hot liquids in silver-rimmed beakers. Another showed a saintly, red headed athlete effortlessly rowing a golden boat through misty waters. A third portrayed a young Roman woman plucking a lyre and a portly, curly-haired poet consulting the Muses, feather-pen in hand. The last one showed two men shaking hands, amicably resolving a grievance. Present behind the life in each mosaic was the god-like personification of Science, Sport, Art and Law. This pantheon governed every student's life in some way, but it was the goddess at the end, the one with the aegis of Minerva around her neck and the palm branch and sword across her lap, that held his attention at the moment. A curious thing he noticed was that she had lost her blindfold. It was lying at her feet. She was staring off into the distance, into the not-so-distant future, seeing everything all at once and, acting not on her own behalf, but as an agent of some one else, deciding the fate of all men.

Trying to make sense of it and of the look that she was now giving him, he said out loud:

"It's God's triage and people fall into one of two categories: those likely to be saved and those not likely to be saved. And *I* fall into—which?"

He looked to her for some indication of where he stood and, after a time she gave him a dubious wink, after which she turned away and wouldn't look at him at all.

"Well," he said to himself. "What did you expect?"

"Not *that*," he admitted. "Even this late in the game, I honestly thought that He'd take pity on me. I thought that maybe— *ah, fuck it!*"

He rushed up the stairs, to the top floor, ran through the labyrinth of stacks to his favorite, private study carrel by the window, overlooking the Northern Quad.

Pressing his face against the large, blackened, plate-glass window, he could see the university buildings laid out across the rolling landscape, like dozens of ornate little puzzle boxes, some flickering in the night, others indistinct in the darkness. When he stepped back, the darkened windowpane turned into a mirror in which he saw the muddled summation of his years spent as a collegian. There were imprints of a cautiously optimistic freshman, naively waiting for the academic world to revolve around him, as he had seen it turn on well-greased ball bearings for freshman of a lighter persuasion. And there were also reflections of a cynical senior trying to reconcile the promise of a college education and everything that drove him out of his fine young mind in pursuit of it.

Taking a few more steps back to broaden his field of view, he searched the glass for what came next, for glimpses of something he had seen in a turn-of-the-century, black and white photograph in the lobby of Dixon Hall. The inscription below the photograph, in an elegant, flowing script, read:

Graduation Day, spring 1926, Father, Son and Young Woman.

To the left was the silver-haired father (*an absentee father, present only for the photo*), a pudgy man in his late 60s, in a sacque suit and Derby hat, a glint of pride behind owlish spectacles. To the right was a pretty girl, the young graduate's fiancé, in an Eton crop hair-do and a French voile dress, her passionate gaze subdued (*a spirited girl, posing, demure until the box-camera flashed*). And the graduate, in an overly starched, button-down shirt, a poorly done necktie and full academic regalia, aware of the occasion's decorum, yet powerless to contain his joy (*a mediocre student, weeping for joy*). What a day it was! A bright day. His best day, because now he'd go home and start a new life.

Sulking by the big window, Juan spoke what his heart most coveted.

"Everything that could not happen will happen now," he said. "I will have everything that they have, everything that their dear Alma Mater, their nurturing mother, gives them. I will graduate *magna cum laude*, my father will come to the ceremony and he will be proud of me. I will be offered a well-paying job straight out of college, be well liked and well respected by my colleagues and by my boss. I will get *the girl* at last. She will want me, love and adore me and marry me. I will live a long, prosperous and happy life, of sound body and *of sound mind . . .*"

But he stopped talking, because he knew that it was crazy talk. He was well aware that he couldn't influence the outcome

218

now. There would be no pomp and circumstance due to certain, unalterable circumstances. And yet here he was again, appealing the decision for the hundredth time, wishing that it would have turned out differently.

He wasn't going home. He was going somewhere else and, by all accounts, was nearly there. In the darkened windowpane, dark as an obsidian mirror, he saw *something*, some solitary thing, moving nimbly along the miles of library aisles, a shadowy tail darting in and out of the dusty stacks, drawing closer to him and him to it.

"*Ah*," said Juan, sounding genuinely surprised, "we've arrived, if I'm not mistaken."

Words to mark his parousia. The long, mournful gongs of Farrington's bells striking midnight confirmed it. His lips parted into a smile and he laughed hysterically. Only then did Juan relax, knowing for once in his life exactly what would happen next.